Mooney's Manifesto

Gregory Gibson

SPUYTEN DUYVIL

New York   Paris

Library of Congress Cataloging-in-Publication Data

Names: Gibson, Gregory, 1945- author.
Title: Mooney's manifesto / Gregory Gibson.
Description: New York ; Paris : Spuyten Duyvil, [2022]
Identifiers: LCCN 2022051670 | ISBN 9781956005905 (paperback)
Classification: LCC PS3607.I2675 M66 2022 | DDC 813.6--dc23
LC record available at https://lccn.loc.gov/2022051670

Against Sisyphusian odds, Greg Gibson keeps his balance, and excellent dialog with himself, strengthened by irony and love of the world, throughout this tragic book depicting a person's Ultimate Struggle with losing an utterly loved son to "random" gun violence. The shocking conclusion of the book will force any reader to come to terms with what really needs to occur to "knock some sense" into a great nation now weighed down with violence, gun-buttery, and very unnecessary tragedies.

Ed Sanders

When somebody tells you a terrible story, calmly, in measured tones, you will never forget where it happened. The only survival technique is to move the action into the landscape, as framed in the screen of a car. I thought when Greg Gibson spoke, both of us looking straight ahead, that writing a book might be the first step towards surviving whatever else was coming in a changed life. *Mooney's Manifesto* is not that story, but it is a spare fiction authenticated and driven by the madness of reality in a country where these things happen. A country that is soon to be everywhere. This is a powerful counterweight to that madness, written out of the sanity of loss and pain, into justified anger.

Ian Sinclair

This book is dedicated to
Curt and Allison Parkingham

"It'll be like dropping a match in a puddle of gasoline."
Joe Mooney

Three summers ago—just before the time of the mosquitoes—I read, in *USA Today*, a front-page article headlined, "Congressman Murdered in Virginia. Two wounded." (At a pro-gun rally, no less. By a crazed bus driver whose daughter and granddaughter had been killed in a domestic violence shooting.) and was shocked to hear myself think, *Now we're getting somewhere!*

That's where my story begins.

LATER JANUARY 3
—THE TIME OF THE MOSQUITOES

The time of the mosquitoes is memorable for one simple reason. No one ever forgets his Damascus moment.

I was sitting in my office in the Book Palace, looking out the window, toward our house across the street. My soon-to-be ex-wife's boyfriend was parked out front. But I wasn't looking at his car or the house. I noticed that two mosquitoes had gotten trapped between the screen and the window, drunk on my blood, no doubt, and were bashing themselves stupidly, repeatedly, against the screen. I started watching them, annoyed at their stupidity, and at my own for watching them. That made me want to destroy them and, by some funny mischance, that urge made me think about the gun in the top drawer of the desk. I thought about the guys down at Smitty's Gun Shop, and about the guns in their showcases, and on their racks and shelves. I thought about where all those guns had come from and where they were bound, and suddenly the sky cracked open and I saw America's gun problem for what it truly was.

There are hardly any animals left to kill, and after a dozen ARs, pistols, shotguns, and rifles, the average collector's acquisitional urges are bound to diminish. The real markets for guns (the last markets left), are soldiers and criminals, and soldiers are getting all the guns they need. The truth is that gun makers make guns for use by bad guys; guns that somehow—by theft or straw purchase or other illegal means—fall into the wrong hands. "Not our fault!" industry people cry. Then they make more guns for people who imagine they need guns to defend themselves against the people who already have guns.

An interesting question came to me then. How come crazed gunmen never go after the people who make the guns? They shoot politicians and they shoot their wives, and they shoot one another. They even shoot themselves, for crying out loud. And cops! There'd been that renewed rash of police assassinations, as I'm sure you recall. In that context, shooting the cynical motherfuckers behind the gun industry didn't seem like much of a leap. It seemed to me that, if you give everyone guns to keep them safe from people with guns, sooner or later they'll start shooting the people who give them the stuff to shoot them with.

It's snowing again—big, fat flakes bashing against my window, stupid as mosquitoes. My fingers wriggle like chubby worms on the keyboard in the glow of the monitor. Just because everything happens for a reason does not mean I am entitled to know that reason—in the moment, or ever. I understand that. Everything happening for a reason simply means the whole thing is a fix, and we drift witless in the mighty system, with only our rage to guide us. Rage is a reason.

It was rage, for example, that led me to Henry Becker. I first saw his toothy face above the fold on the front page of the *New York Times*, braying about the passage of the law legalizing universal concealed carry.

"There's a big tailwind we have, moving from state legislature to state legislature. The South, the Midwest, I knew we could pass this law in those states."

What a victory! Now anyone can carry a pistol anywhere. All those untrained, ignorant people with pistols stuck in their pants, enabled by that NRA jackass, Henry Becker.

As I beheld his smarmy, self-satisfied puss there arose in me a very particular sort of anger—calm, itself concealed, but knowing no bounds. His image occasioned the creation of my most enduring fantasy loop. Becker is cowering in the corner of his office, begging me to stop. I bring the pistol right up to his face, which is streaming with snot and tears. *Now do you see what it's like? The last moment of a life?* The hot stink of his involuntary fecal purge hovers over us.

Over and over, almost as if I were praying.

One thing I can't stand—actually, there are a lot more than one and I suppose I *do* stand them. Though I *would* like to take those myriad intolerable things and line them up against a wall and…

It's funny, the way figures of speech work.

One thing that really annoys me is novels about parents whose children have died. Dennis Ford's *The Sportswriter* comes to mind. I can't tell you how many people pressed that book into my hands after my son's murder. They knew I was a big reader and they thought… I don't know what they thought. Maybe that reading a book about a guy with a dead son would give me something to do while I sat around having a dead son. Certainly, it was a book that impressed them, those well-meaning book pressers, and I know they recommended it because they cared about me. Could they have imagined that reading this tale of, what was his name? Frank? That reading this story about Frank Bascombe would somehow cheer me up? Mitigate my suffering? Improve my life? Maybe it was just so they'd have a way to talk with me about Ryan's death without having to talk about the way he died. It must be awful, having to talk to someone like me. I could feel it during the first weeks I dared venture from my house. Walking down the Snacks & Soda aisle at the supermarket, my townspeople carefully not gawking at their own worst nightmare.

Richard, not Dennis. That novelist's name was Richard Ford.

Barbara Jackson's son was shot and killed two months after Ryan. Except her son, Cooper, was gunned down on the mean streets of the ghetto rather than the leafy environs of a college campus. I first met Barbara on the gun control speaking circuit. Every gun violence prevention rally featured speeches from people who'd had loved ones shot and killed. Our stories were intended to inspire those true believers (though their kind attentions more likely to inspire us to keep battling the bottomless grief that seemed perpetually on the brink of devouring us). Her speeches were simple and direct. Erect. From the heart, and spiced with the slightest lilt of a West Indian accent. You felt her pain (we were all very good at communicating pain), but somehow she was able to impart a bright and clear sense of the fundamental *wrongness* of gun violence. People were too good to keep letting it happen. Therefore it must cease.

She and I were serving dinners at Trauma Night in the basement of the Church of Zion and she told me, "People get so awkward talking about Cooper."

"Yeah, they think they're going to hurt you, open up old wounds."

"But I like it when they talk about him. Kind of brings him back."

She's a lovely person, Barbara. Round black face in a bed of tight gray curls on a head constantly tilted back like she's checking you out, like she can't quite get what you're about, but that whatever it is, it makes her smile. I don't know what she was like before her son was killed, but grief has not made her a meaner or less tolerant person. A while back someone gave me a *New Yorker* article about living through a traumatic event, how it might have some positive effects. Not that you'd suffer or grieve less, but that the experience could make you more understanding and compassionate. I don't mind people pressing that kind of reading into my hands.

But Ford's sportswriter, Bascombe, and his fey, coy, indecisiveness. What a load of shit. It was all so novelistic. Though I have to admit, the part where he interviews the old athlete was pretty good. Maybe there were other good parts. My annoyance has wiped them out.

Except for this—and it holds for every other novel involving dead children, and for every review those novels invariably receive, praising their humanity and courage. As if the reviewers knew what they were talking about. They've never had their kids killed. But they collaborate with novelists in the business of creating and marketing stories. Despicable when you think about it that way, because what they're really doing is appropriating—for entertainment purposes— the agony of anyone who has survived a murdered child. Appropriating *my* agony, for example.

I wrote about the experience of losing Ryan, some earlier parts of it, in a memoir called *Goodbye, My Son,* which was published by Horizon House who, incidentally, are real publishers, not a vanity press. My anger at college officials for not stopping the shooter stoked my curiosity about how such a thing could have happened. But it was also a coming-of-age story about Ryan, and about our relationship. The book received reviews praising its humanity and courage.

Still, it was only a book, no more than selected shapely bits from the story that is my life, the story that does not end on the last page of any book. So many things have happened since that page!

Would you believe that someone as crazy as Ryan's

killer could walk into a gun shop right now and buy an assault rifle just as easily as he did back in the day?

Since Ryan's death I've spent years closely watching nothing happen. Or watching a lot happen, most of which involves people getting killed by guns and politicians doing nothing about it. Politics, friends, has degenerated into mere performance, while governance takes place in venues unseen by us, beyond our control. Corporations conspire with murky global interests and the gun—that terrible, brutal, crucial gun—operates on their behalf as the delivery system for the consequences of racism, poverty, injustice, and the madness they inspired.

And we drift witless in the mighty system.

I might flatter myself that my perspective is unique, but my story is not. Since Ryan's death six years ago, a quarter of a million more people have been killed by guns in America. That's right—250,000 dead. And for each of those dead ones there are, what—ten or a dozen fathers, mothers, brothers, sisters, lovers and friends? Millions of people each year whose lives have been turned to shit by a gun.

When my colleagues and fellow survivors hear why I did what I did, they'll know what to do. And they'll have plenty to do it with. There are 400 million guns floating around in this country right now, and they're not going away any time soon.

It's like a hole opening up.

JANUARY 5
—ROBOTS

According to a disappointingly brief article buried in the middle of this morning's *New York Times* "Officials Remain Mum on Holiday Shootings." Whoever says "mum" in real life?

Three weeks and I'm off the front page.

They seem to have figured out that the murders are related in some way, but God, it's tortuous. I feel sorry for the newspapers, trying so hard, always falling behind Twitter, slowly starving, getting skinnier and skinnier. That's why I try to support them. *Wall Street Journal* and *Rockledge Courier* delivered each morning. *New York Times* and *USA Today* on my daily walk down to 7-Eleven.

Of course, I'm dying to know if they're really on to me, those mum ones, and if the "monstrous" acts I perpetrated against Becker and those others have yet had their effect on the American psyche. Could that be why they're keeping a lid on this thing? Once people understand why it happened, it will happen again. It will. And again.

Meanwhile, a bizarre op-ed in *USA Today* has given me a great idea for a science fiction story. The piece was called "Why Waste More Money on Science?" and the gist was that our experiments with artificial intelligence would soon escape us. Robots would no longer be under our control. All our efforts to halt global warming, to end terrorism, to rid the planet of nuclear weapons—all our well-meaning attempts to make the world a better place—were futile because artificial intelligence would soon be in control of us. What we needed to do, the writer said, was stop all this research and take a long look at where we were headed.

But I thought, *Great! Let the robots take over. They'll be more rational than humans, incapable of greed, lust, and selfishness. No more fanaticism. The robots take control of the world, and they'll end global warming and nuclear weapons. They'll save the planet for us. Save the planet from us.*

According to my calendar today is Epiphany, which is perfect.

Our big old house across the street is wrapped in dusky gloom, but the very top of the maple in the front yard, right above Ryan's window, is high enough to catch the last rays of the setting sun, and its naked branches ripple red and orange in the breeze, as if they were on fire. I don't want to make it sound easy. It was not easy. Sitting in my dead son's room was not easy. Watching the clock not move was not easy. Not wanting to live was not easy. You wonder how people survive such things.

Six months, a year, two and three years—the pain kept not going away. I had grieved before, but this was different. For Bethany it was somatic. Ryan was a piece of her. Can you imagine learning in the most direct and memorable manner that the world is a cruel, unfeeling place in which the thing you love most can be torn from you at any instant, for no reason you will ever discern? I suffered, in my own way, all the things my wife suffered, and I felt the pain of her pain. At the same time though, she gave me a sense of purpose; I had to care for her.

Bethany appreciated my attentiveness, my capering, my patience. My sweetie and I were going down this road together—at least until I got wrapped up in my gun studies. Still, there was a part of our grief, a deep and mysterious part, that our mutual ministrations could not touch, that time seemed unable to heal. I've witnessed it in others over the years. We endure a grief so unrelenting and omnipresent that life seems made of grief, and we have no idea why.

But looking back now, I think I know.

That first night, when the midnight call came, as I squeezed the phone and listened to that nitwit administrator's voice dribble out, telling me there'd been a "terrible accident" at the college and that Ryan was dead, and Bethany was behind me, saying "No..." softly, over and over, I had a vision. I saw, right before me in the darkened hallway—but I felt it as well—a glowing, two-pronged fork. The prong to the left went into the dark and vanished. That was the life we would have led, with Ryan in it. The prong on the right was a throbbing stub—the beginning of this new life without Ryan.

It took a long while to fully grasp the meaning of that vision. We'd lost Ryan and, in the most basic and profound way, our lives would never be the same. With his death our own lives, our old lives, also died. We were grieving for ourselves as well as for Ryan, but we didn't know it. That was why we could never find the bottom of our grief.

That was my epiphany, anyway, taking a walk this afternoon, looking up at a dark flock of birds against the wintry sky, swooping and darting as if they were a single bird, but with no one bird leading them. There's a word for that kind of flock, I know. I watched the pulsing mass of them, and I thought, *We're grieving for ourselves and we don't even know it.*

JANUARY 6

Every once in a while, I'll be making a cup of coffee or trying to decide which shirt to wear, and something will come over me and I'll stop and look out into space, which is to say into the world, which somehow resides in that space into which I am looking, and become lost in or bear witness to the overwhelming complexity of it, almost as if I were praying, but to what? Then I'll pick out the day's shirt.

Janine was Bethany's mentor in woman's studies, astrology, and feminine arts beyond my ken. A handsome, fiery woman whose accent betrayed her Brooklyn Irish origins, Janine had put her divorce settlement to good use operating an art gallery called Wild Iris. Bethany was the slinky Vassar grad in the black turtleneck at the front desk, and Janine's boyfriend Hank lurked about, adding to the Beatnik ambiance of the place. He'd gone to Columbia and had fallen in with Patti Smith and her crowd, though they didn't impress him as much as they impressed the rest of the world. Not much impressed Hank, and we assumed that his impassiveness was the mark of the true, original Beatnik. He had stories, if you could extract them. And he could draw like an angel.

In keeping with the ambiance, Janine eschewed lighthouses and sailboats in favor of abstract art, which hardly anyone bought, which made Wild Iris more like a coffee house than an art gallery. Every Saturday night she and Hank would clear the back wall of paintings and show classic movies. Tuesday nights featured live performances of jazz and folk music. Wednesday nights were chess nights, and on Thursday nights open mic adventures ran the gamut from poetry to comedy to performance art, with frequent inadvertent collisions of genres. There was a lot of talent around and the tip jar was usually overflowing.

College had soured me on academia. For reasons that escape me, but possibly simply because I was a young idiot, I did two years of postgraduate work in the Marine Corps, a forgettable interlude marked primarily by my learning to fold my shirts, field strip an M16, and address civilians as "Ma'am" and "Sir." Subsequently, in hopes of redeeming the time I'd wasted serving my country, I spent another two years producing an unpublishable novel about a young Marine, and bales of incomprehensible poetry, mostly reflections upon the complexity of life as experienced by a young ex-Marine. Some of this I read, to good effect, on Thursday night open mic sessions at Wild Iris. Incomprehensibility did not deter that crowd. Janine and Hank and I became fast friends and, in nearly as little time, Bethany and I became an item, much to Janine's delight.

One day Janine said, "You've always liked books. Why don't you sell old books in my gallery?"

"What about the art?"

"We've got too much art. We need more life."

I didn't need more convincing. I quit my jobs washing dishes, driving taxis, and painting houses, and built some shelves in Janine's gallery. She fronted me $500, and we set up as business partners. Back then, $500 bought a lot of used books. When it was time to price our wares, the range was 50¢ to $5 (which appeared to be the upper limit of what the market would bear). People began poking through our shelves and making purchases. It was brilliant. We'd buy stuff and they'd come in and buy it from us, and we'd take the money they gave us for the stuff and use it to buy more stuff, which they would then obligingly buy.

On the strength of this happy scenario Janine closed the art gallery and moved the books into a bigger space. Our retail business saw a healthy increase. Then an ugly, Malthusian sort of fact reared its head. Our seaside town, though picturesque, had a year-round population insufficient to generate enough income to support two people. It felt grand in the summer when tourists poured through like spawning pogies, but each year there came a day in October when everything stopped. You could almost hear it—a grinding, crunching sound that meant seven months of anxiety and poverty. Janine took note of this and wisely moved out of town, leaving me on my own.

That's not true. I forced her out.

She was a valued adviser and beloved auntie to both Bethany and me, but I'd come to realize that book dealing was going to be my life's work, and that for Janine it would never be anything but an aesthetic adventure. She was wise enough to recognize this fundamental difference of intent and, before our fights could become too damaging, she decamped for a new life in Brattleboro, Vermont, where one of her grown sons lived, taking the name Wild Iris with her, and leaving me at liberty to establish Joseph Mooney Rare Books, Inc.

Bethany was bereft. Janine came back for visits, and we took road trips to Brattleboro but, as our new lives swallowed us, the old Wild Iris days receded into legend. Janine's departure, her abandonment of us, ossified into a sadness that Bethany stored in the sadness bin with her many other sadnesses.

Then, wonder of wonders, Bethany got pregnant.

This caused the shit, as we used to say in the Corps, to hit the fan. We were young and brave and deeply in love, excited by the prospect of starting a family together. Wasn't that enough? It was not. At least not in the eyes of Bethany's parents, Curt and Allison Parkingham, solid, well-to-do folks (he owned car dealerships in north Jersey). College degree and military service notwithstanding, I was neither a doctor, a lawyer, nor a business chief, and was therefore unqualified to get into their daughter's pants. The fact that I saw no reason to get married was the final straw for them.

Once Bethany and I became convinced that a shotgun could and would be produced, we assented to a shotgun wedding. It was a melancholy affair, performed by our local justice of the peace, after his morning round of golf, under a tree across the street from City Hall, attended by the Parkinghams (both my parents had died years before) and by Janine and Hank who were witness to the proceedings, followed by an exquisitely uncomfortable lunch at a local tavern. The bill, with tip, came to something less than $250. I got a glimpse of it before Mr. Parkingham scooped it up. I'd just saved the man $50,000 on a fancy wedding, and all he could do was glower at me.

Bethany had a frightening delivery and was bedridden for months, during which time she suffered an even-more-frightening bout of postpartum depression. Eventually it lifted, or so I thought. Much later (too late!) I realized it had never gone away.

This difficult stretch was followed by years of Bethany, Ryan, and me figuring out how to make that Jerry-built contraption called "a family" work. It didn't come with instructions. We had our insights, made our compromises, and managed—thanks mostly to Ryan— to have a pretty good time of it. He was fast and wriggly, and a natural comedian. As he matured, he added mimicry to his talents, along with a preternatural knack for retaining movie dialog after only a single hearing. These abilities made him popular with his peers, and our house in those days was always full of kids. I think he missed having a sibling. We all did. So we took in half a dozen of them, both sexes. And if, perhaps, they drank, smoked pot, or engaged in other illicit activities in the abandoned shack across the street, at least we could keep an eye on them. It was a wonderful growing up. For all of us.

The summer before Ryan started high school it

became apparent that my career path as the quirky proprietor of a quaint used book shop would ultimately result in my committing assault and battery on some hapless idiot for asking if I could do better on a price, or who told me that he'd have to come back when he had more time. I was out of time. For his kind, anyway.

I dumped my retail business, bought and restored that shack across from our house just in time to save it from falling into the ground, ejected Ryan and his pals, and installed Janine's old boyfriend Hank (who'd been helping me at the shop for years) at a desk with a computer, surrounded by the finest pickings of my stock. Thus, the old shack began its second life as my Book Palace. Browsers were forbidden. Now the game was rare book shows, librarians' conferences, catalogs of select merchandise mailed to select customers, and regular email blasts listing my latest finds. I'll spare you the discussion of how much of this was ego driven—the Joseph Mooney Rare Peacock Show, as Hank liked to call it—and how much was genuine intellectual curiosity.

Suffice it to say that, as I sit here tonight, surrounded by the fruits and consequences of my hard-fought years in the trade, I can at least congratulate myself on having progressed from being a mere used book seller to a genuine antiquarian book dealer. If mine isn't the most expensive material on the market (I scorn mere trophy-hunting) my goods are always interesting and, occasionally, irresistible to some institutional library or wealthy collector.

Now that the digital age is upon us devices and smart phones rule. The book—that stack of printed paper, folded and sewn—has lost its primary function as a container and transmitter of information. It survives mostly as an artifact, as a repository of childhood memories, as a symbol of wealth, as an *object of desire*. I adapted my business to this trend, concentrating on quirky, rare material that would always, I hoped, be desirable. Now, I bragged, "I buy things that don't exist and sell them to people who don't know they want them."

A flawed business model, alas. Every nickel I make in books seems to go right back into the purchase of increasingly obscure and desirable rarities. And, while I'm feeding on myself financially, I am simultaneously backing into a niche so rarefied as to be virtually non-existent. It has taken me most of my career to comprehend what should be obvious to the greenest tyro: rare stuff is rare—difficult to find—because there isn't much of it, which is what "rare" means. As a result, my rare book dealings have lately been reduced to a trickle of high-end transactions. But I can't stop. Don't want to stop. Don't need to stop.

The truth is, I never did much more than break even in the hunt for objects of desire. It was Curt and Allison Parkingham who helped Bethany and me buy our comfortable old house in Rockledge, pay our bills, and see to Ryan's upbringing and education. They kept us solvent after Ryan's death, when we were too shattered to do anything, and they continued paying the bills while I wandered up and down the country, interviewing people who would become characters in my humane and courageous memoir. I should have dedicated *Goodbye, My Son* to Curt and Allison. It just seemed awkward having their names on the same page as Ryan's.

JANUARY 8
—THE KILLER

Ryan's killer was a kid named Richard Winters. He showed up at school from West Texas in a tweed jacket with leather elbow patches, under the grievously mistaken impression that he'd be attending an Ivy League college. In fact, the place was a hotbed of drug addicts, hippies, and homos. Or so it seemed to him. The boys had green hair and the girls had no hair at all. Richard might have been highly intelligent, but he'd been raised in a rigidly structured environment, long on Jesus and short on deviance. No one had prepared him for the inversions and experiments he'd encounter at a small east coast liberal arts college. Brier Hill was listed near the top in the annual rankings of American colleges—small school division—in *Newsweek Magazine*. That was all they knew back home.

Even if he'd been stable and resilient the shock of landing in Brier Hill might have overwhelmed him. But he was neither stable nor resilient. He snapped just before Christmas. The Supreme Being had a mission for him. He was ordered to punish the transgressors, to cleanse the college of its deviant filth.

He smuggled his rifle onto campus in a guitar

case, having bought it, used, at a local sporting goods store—a perfectly legal purchase at the time. High-capacity magazines and ammo came from a gun show in Vermont and were transported across state lines in Richard's backpack on a Peter Pan bus. What a ride that must've been! One of his associates, with whom he'd been having increasingly agitated conversations about guns and gun shows, sensed something weird going on, and soon there was a rumor afloat that Dickie-do was armed and dangerous. The Dean of Students decided he'd better get to the bottom of the matter, and went around to Winters's room to question him personally about this gun nonsense. Despite the fact that he was in the midst of a full-blown psychotic break, the Dickster had sense enough to hide his gun, and little trouble convincing the clueless Dean that the thirty-round magazines under his desk were Christmas gifts for this father.

Little Richard went out that evening and positioned himself on the hill above the entrance to the auditorium. When the Christmas concert ended and the crowd streamed out, he started shooting, killing four and wounding six. People sometimes tell me how tragic it was that Ryan happened to be in the wrong place at the wrong time. I think this is intended as consolation, but it makes me furious. Richard Winters was in the wrong place, not Ryan Mooney. But is that even what they mean? Doesn't "wrong" imply some kind of fault? Ryan's entire life delivered him to that last fatal place at the last fatal moment. Did that mean he'd lived it in error? Whenever they spout that wrong place nonsense I mumble and turn away, feigning grief. Maybe next time I'll just sucker punch my informant, splattering his nose like a ripe pomegranate.

Anyway, here's where it gets strange. Stranger.

Most of these lunatics bring their orgies to a climax by shooting themselves. But something different happened to the crazed Dickhead. The cheap aftermarket magazine of his carbine worked loose and became improperly seated. The bullets stopped cycling and the newbie psycho killer did not know how to clear the jam. Just at this moment, perhaps not coincidentally, the florid phase of his psychosis let up. God went off to take another call and the young man found himself standing outside the auditorium with a smoking gun in his hands. Whereupon he did what any law-abiding citizen would do when he sees something wrong occurring—he went in a dorm and called the police. And by some miracle the call got through. They played that 911 tape on the news so often the whole country must have heard it. *I just shot some people at Brier Hill College.* That Texas twang of his. In short order the local constabulary arrived. Richard threw down his gun, raised his hands in the air and, by yet another miracle, was not shot. Disappointed SWAT teams returned to their lairs.

Thus, he proved to be a rarity—a mass shooter who'd survived his shooting. The poor kid couldn't get anything right. On the other hand, he was guaranteed a lifetime as a lab rat for psychologists, newscasters and documentary film makers. Paradise for any narcissistic psychopath.

Another strange thing took place that night. Maybe even miraculous, depending on how you look at it. Richard Winters had expended most of a thirty-round magazine when the gun malfunctioned. Ryan had been the last person shot. As I watched the news clips of distraught parents rushing onto campus and embracing their terrified children, all I could think about was the many lives that had been saved by that single, jammed bullet—the one after the one that had killed my son. The needle kept wavering back and forth over the red line. You go crazy if you think about that stuff long enough.

JANUARY 8
—COCKTAIL HOUR

I know. I need to tell you about Becker, Freedman and Sawtelle, those cynical slaughterers of innocents, and how I came to choose them. Though, if I hadn't seen them for what they were, someone else would have. Others, I'm certain, already have. Or soon will. Or ones exactly like them, those three stooges. Of whom, God knows, there are plenty more than three.

I need to explain to you exactly why those gun-peddling bastards deserved every bit of what they got. And I will. But you must indulge me. These recollections, as they begin to spin out through dark afternoons and darker evenings, seem so inviting. I pull one up and find another attached to it. The whiskey keeps tasting better.

Even though he was manifestly guilty, Winters still had to be tried for his crimes in a court of law. Which was where things got difficult. Or, more complicated than difficult. Or, difficult at first then revealing themselves as complex, these "things" to which I refer. Because these things are no more or less than the events of our lives which, if you trouble yourself to examine them, demonstrate in short order that the fundamental nature of life is complexity. So, difficult first, then becoming complex, which is to say more imbued with life.

The wheels of justice turn slowly, or grind slowly, or whatever it is they're supposed to do, and they don't much care about the anguish their slowness inflicts upon the victims of the crime they are adjudicating. In Winters's case all sorts of additional nonsense came up. There was a fight over the venue, whether the sensational nature of the crime would allow for a fair trial in its original jurisdiction. (You could hear me in the solitude of the book Palace screaming FAIR TRIAL?) These delays were hard to bear, but they were harder still on those near and dear to us. I began to worry about them.

Sounds funny, I know. But unless you've been in that situation, you can't imagine. We were determined to go to this trial, to sit in the seats up front, to represent Ryan, so that the people who were the agents of those impersonal, slowly grinding wheels would not forget that a handsome, promising, and blameless young man had been killed for no reason other than the ease with which a nut had been able to get his hands on a gun. The judge, the reporters, Richard Winters's public defender, the Dean of Students at Brier Hill who'd been hoodwinked by a madboy—they needed to see us sitting there.

Our supporters, however, assumed that we were subjecting ourselves to this ordeal because the trial, and our attendance at it, would give us "closure"—a fantasy they could hardly be blamed for entertaining, besotted as they were with good advice from Oprah and Dr. Phil. "Closure" was supposed to seal the deal. Once this kid was locked away for life all accounts would be settled and Bethany and I could then begin "healing." Perhaps, if we were sufficiently enlightened, we'd strive for the brass ring of "forgiveness," though that wasn't a mandatory step. Mostly, our attainment of "closure" would mean that they wouldn't have to worry about us as much anymore.

Finally, the court scheduled a real trial date and, as it approached, our friends would not leave us alone. Messages of encouragement flooded in. Hot meals, now. Bethany was surrounded by her parents and her flock of weeping angels, and their ranks were supplemented by kindly neighbors, and by distant friends and relatives, all of whom had our backs. Though it felt more like they were breathing down our necks.

That was when I got the idea to send out email bulletins for the benefit of our well-wishers. I had already decided that, as long as I was going to be in the courtroom six hours a day for three weeks, I might as well keep busy by taking notes. I was quite conscious of the drama inherent in the situation and I thought that my account of the trial, published in one of the major newspapers, might be a vehicle for my revenge upon the dopes at Brier Hill College who'd let all this happen. So I brought a steno pad with me and assiduously recorded everything I saw, heard, felt, and thought, which carried me far beyond the pettiness of vengeful newspaper articles. You wouldn't believe how much there was to write. So strange, so ceremonious, so intricate!

Bethany and I went back to our hotel that first night, and while she wept and napped, I typed up the day's notes and tried to organize them into some kind of coherent narrative. Same thing the next day, and the next. Saturday afternoon I emailed my report of the week's proceedings to our friends. These bulletins served their purpose well enough, but something unexpected happened in the process.

I wasn't suffering anymore.

I mean, of course I was suffering, but the quality of that suffering had changed. I was no longer the anguished father of a murdered child, because now I was reporting on the trial. As a part of that activity, I was also reporting on the father sitting at the trial, the parent who'd once been me but was now a reporter reporting on himself and everything around him in the courtroom, comforting his wife in their hotel, slamming down whiskeys after "work," spending hours each evening transcribing his notes, and more hours the next morning polishing them before going off to harvest more notes.

I'd ceased being a victim and had become a reporter.

That was the engine that powered the story that made my book. Becoming a reporter saved my life, I'm convinced. It helped me save Bethany's, and it paved the way for *Goodbye, My Son.*

JANUARY 8
—THE WHOLE OMELET

Wrong, wrong, wrong. Not about the reporting, but about the book, which proved, in a truly heartbreaking way, to be the mother of all wrong turns. I wasted years curating my humane and courageous story in hopes that it would change America's mind about guns. America remained unmoved. But I've learned, of necessity, to be patient with myself. When you break an egg, clean up the mess.

I knew my story would have to sound like more than a police report, so I mined my tough-guy fantasies for scraps of a persona and welded them together with rage. This character's voice was like a truth-seeking missile. A son's murder was its power, its authority. No one could dismiss it. Just like in the supermarket, it spoke people's living nightmare; living their nightmare. While I was attending to the creation and maintenance of that voice, the events it narrated rolled out of their own accord.

I went on the road and talked to guys who sold guns in gun shops. I confronted the head of the college. I talked to Ryan's friends and teachers. I talked to the killer's—well, sociopaths don't have friends, so I guess you'd call them associates. I even talked to the killer's parents, Billy and Doreen Winters. Good, honest, heartbroken rednecks.

They were the ones who brought the piece the book needed. Their fundamental decency punched through my tough-guy pretensions and made me understand that I should portray every character with respect, even the administrators at the college, cloistered idiots though they were. Life is difficult for all of us, and you have to treat people with respect for the difficulties they endure, even if they're only characters in a story.

A guy I grew up with had become a successful writer, and he helped a lot, reading version after version of chapter after chapter, guiding me through the rudiments of storytelling, but generally hanging back, waiting to see what I could make of the thing stuck inside me.

I'd go out and do an interview and come home and write it up, then mope about in a state of emotional exhaustion until the life force came back into me— manifesting itself initially as rage—upon which I'd go back out and repeat the cycle. When there were no more people to talk to and no more rage to fuel me, *Goodbye, My Son* was finished.

Bethany and I flew out to Los Angeles for a short

stay with my writer pal, who would not say much about my book except that it "had a shot," which I thought was an odd choice of words. He drove me to an intimidatingly fancy hotel down the street from where O.J. Simpson had once lived, and took me up to meet his agent, who happened to be in town conducting agent business. She was a skinny strawberry blonde about my age, in shorts and a blouse, with surprising red toenails, reclining in a recliner in the sun on the deck by the David Hockney swimming pool that, for some LA reason, was on the roof of this hotel, rather than on the ground where pools belonged. A white-coated Latino appeared. The agent ordered a mango smoothie and recommended the same to us. I listened attentively while the waiter ran through the list of healthy delights available for our consumption, then ordered a double bourbon straight up, water back. I thought my drink choice made a statement consonant with the voice of the guy telling the story in the book that I wanted her to represent. But when the waiter delivered our drinks, I thoughtlessly glugged my bourbon down all at once. Then, in the California sun, by the side of that surreal twenty-seventh floor pool in the fancy hotel down the street from O.J.'s pad, I became excessively light headed, unable to comprehend what the agent was telling me about my writing, though I did get the impression that she was too big-time to represent a little book like mine. My west coast writer pal was pretty big-time himself, so I don't suppose I should have expected anything else. But he was a kind man at heart, and his agent wound up being kindly, too. She sent me a letter soon after our interview referring me to another agent, a colleague of hers, who she thought might be a good fit for me and my book.

So I went down to New York, into the offices of Meyer Creative, and introduced myself to Daniel, a nervous, goateed little fellow with a prominent Adam's apple and sparkling, button-like eyes, who immediately said, "We can sell this!" causing me, of course, to sign with Meyer Creative—15% off the top—whereupon Daniel and I set out to test his "We can sell this!" assessment which, surprisingly, turned out to be correct. We got three offers, the best of which came from Horizon House. I asked him if he thought he could get them up a little more. He said the money was damned good for a first book by an unknown. $7500! I would have done it for nothing.

Time Magazine called my memoir "Courageous and humane—must reading for anyone interested in America's plague of gun violence." *Entertainment Weekly* named it one of the best non-fiction books of the year.

Encouraged by favorable critical responses, Horizon hired a publicist who sent me to Atlanta, Washington, New York, and Boston. I had soulful conversations with Ellen on the Ellen Show and with Leonard Lopate in New York and Chris Lydon in Boston, and with dozens of drive-time radio moron jocks who hadn't read my book, couldn't read.

Then she sent me to the west coast. For my two days in southern California she provided me with a big Nigerian dude named Douglas. These handlers—I think they're referred to in the trade as "author escorts"—are independent contractors who guide touring authors from one place to the next. Douglas wore an immaculately pressed black suit with a violet shirt open at the collar. He drove me around in his Buick to indies like Vromans and Book Soup. I'd barge into the store, introducing myself to the manager, then rushing over to where my books were displayed—in my case it was usually "Parenting" or "Grief and Grieving," hardly ever "True Crime"—and signing as many copies as I could before they threw me out. If they didn't have my book, I'd flash the *Entertainment Weekly* review praising my humanity and courage.

Douglas and I had a ball. He told tales of poorly behaved authors (though he did speak highly of

Richard Ford, that novelist of dead sons). We went to Musso and Frank's for lunch, and they *knew* him there. He said he'd been a Prince back home, and I told him I'd never known a Nigerian who wasn't. We ordered another drink.

Oh, I was in tall cotton back then. It was, as they say, like a dream. I was supporting my family by flogging my book. I was honoring Ryan and, even more importantly, Ryan and I were putting an end to gun violence by courageously sharing our story. Once people understood the manner in which the ripples of suffering spread, ultimately affecting us all, they would rise as one and put a stop to the insane proliferation of firearms. Hardly ever at home, paying no mind to Bethany or my rare book business, living in the moment, going around telling people, "Gun violence happens wherever there are guns, and guns are everywhere." I'd warn them, "Don't let it happen to you," supposedly referring to my having a school-murdered son on account of insane gun laws and lame-assed, head-in-the-sand college administrators, but actually, poignantly, and unbeknownst to myself, referring to my own predicament, which involved a steadily worsening and inappropriate relationship with the story that was my life.

My time on the road brought more positive notices which got me gigs as a talking head on TV news shows, analyzing subsequent mass shootings of which, I don't need to tell you, there were plenty. The earnest host would say, "With us today is Joseph Mooney, author of *Goodbye, My Son,* a memoir about the death of his son in a school shooting." After a while he or she would ask, in an anguished tone of voice, "How can this keep happening?" The light over my camera would go on and I'd say, "Because it's so easy to get guns, that's how." Simple, direct, and intuitively, if not grammatically, correct. I'd spend the rest of my allotted 60 seconds explaining that the epidemic of gun violence needed to be treated as a public health problem rather than as a battle over the meaning of the Second Amendment. My closing zinger was, "If this is the price our children must pay for a freedom their elders enjoy, we need to re-examine the contract."

I wrote letters, too, identifying myself as the author of the well-known memoir, and urging Congressmen and Senators to do something about lax gun laws and loopholes. Senator Perkins, from our state, was a big help. He allowed me to drop his name at will. Once I wrote a letter to Governor Chase, chastising him for an insensitive remark he made about "lunatics with assault rifles and oversized clips blowing people away." He surprised me by apologizing to me in person and in a public statement that got a lot of air play. He'd made his offensive remark, he said, because he had not been educated about the problem. The first step is education, he told us. Education and awareness. Once we realize there's a problem, we can begin working together to find a solution.

I was tempted to ask how clueless one had to be not see there's a problem when 40,000 people die each year. If Monkey Pox killed 40,000 Americans, we'd sure as hell know we had a problem. But I have to give the Governor credit, he showed some class. How many politicians ever admit a mistake? It was a civilized, gracious thing to do, and his theme of education and awareness resonated with people. He won by a slim margin that fall—did I mention that he was in the midst of a tough re-election campaign? The next thing I knew I was on the stage when he made his inaugural address, in which he mentioned, with a nod in my direction, "the terrible cost of gun violence to families and communities across our state."

Such was the pride that wenteth before my fall. I

should've known something was up when the publicist called and told me her gig with Horizon House was at an end. We got a little weepy on the phone and swore we'd stay in touch. Of course, I never heard from her again. Not that I tried to call her, either. I had her numbers, but I was busy.

I did a talk at a boy's prep school in Baltimore. They all wore sweaters and ties. Then a convention of humorless (they didn't laugh at any of my introductory jokes) Victim Service providers, and a seminar on threat assessment in DC, thanks to the Senator, then three colleges in a row. Two of them were community colleges, the toughest crowds I'd ever had. It was June, just before school let out for the year. Those kids didn't care that I was the father of a murdered son who'd published a courageous and humane memoir. They didn't give a damn who I was.

That set the tone for the rest of my career as a famous author. I had a wonderful new idea about a state-wide billboard campaign, but I couldn't even get a call returned from the Governor or the Senator's offices. At the end of the summer, I went down to New York to meet with my editor and the sales people at Horizon to talk about plans for a paperback edition.

I was hungover and too full of coffee and, as a result,

I'm afraid I acted in an imperious manner, the big-shot author of the well-reviewed memoir, who hung out with governors and senators. Why wasn't I getting a publicist and a tour for the paperback? Why were they planning such a teeny print run? And where was the advertising? All of a sudden, I heard myself and stopped.

My editor said, "The returns are in. We've got some numbers."

"And?"

"Not so good, I'm afraid. Nearly six thousand returns so far. Ten thousand warehoused. We've sold about two thousand copies, total."

I didn't know much about publishing, but I knew enough to understand that those numbers represented a crushing, humiliating failure. The book hadn't even "earned out" my advance. No surprise, then, that the paperback edition died aborning. Who'd want to buy a $12.95 soft cover when you could get the first edition hardcover for $0.99 at any of the remainder houses? Who'd even want to read about a murdered son in the first place? It was a bummer. A nightmare. The critics who'd given us those good reviews had been paid to read it. No one else, it seemed, could be bothered.

I went home to grieve.

Bethany had words of consolation. She told me I'd

helped raise national awareness about gun violence, wasn't that an accomplishment? But I wasn't having any. My failure was inescapable, my humiliation complete. Gun violence was rolling along just fine despite my best efforts. (That awful convent shooting in Elmhurst, Illinois happened just about then. I remember the *Enquirer* being censured for its BLOODY MARY headline.) When I went over to the Book Palace Hank did not offer consolation. He grunted and barely looked up from his desk, which was a relief.

Sometimes it almost seems accidental. A patch of black ice, and next thing you know you're rolling on the sidewalk, screaming in agony, clutching your shattered elbow.

We tend to think of rare book dealers (if we think about them at all) as a refined lot of connoisseurs. But some of the legendary ones, though gifted with prodigious memories and deep, instinctive understandings of the human psyche, could barely read. The best one I know can read well enough, but he avoids the tweedy trappings of our trade.

His name is Andy Willets and, instead of luxuriating in a Book Palace full of rare tomes, as I do, he works out of a beat-up Chevy. Andy uses a tablet to comb online listings of country auctions and, while traveling from auction to auction, visits flea markets, railroad conventions, yard sales, Civil War re-enactments, gun, coin, and stamp shows, book shops, and antique malls anywhere and everywhere east of the Mississippi. When he's done for the day, he goes on Priceline or Hotels.com and finds a place to sleep on the cheap. His diet consists mostly of whiskey and chocolate-covered coffee beans, and he completes the *New York Times* crossword puzzle each morning in minutes. In pen. He's as close to a genius as anyone I've ever known. He's also a major source for the rare books and manuscripts I so desire.

I remember that particular Sunday evening as if it were yesterday. I was on my way home from an antiquarian book fair in Albany, New York when I got a call from Andy. He was headed west from the famed flea markets in Brimfield, Massachusetts, where he'd discovered a journal of an 1846 whaling voyage in which the captain who was writing it recorded his dreams and, ultimately, his descent into madness. Very exotic stuff! The price was steep, but I how could I resist?

We met at a Cracker Barrel restaurant off the New York Thruway. Like most establishments of its kind. this one was full of large people, some of whom needed walkers to haul themselves from one place to the next. It called itself a "family-style restaurant," which meant no alcohol, so our meeting was shorter than it might otherwise have been.

He asked what I'd been up to.

"You know I bought up the remainders of *Goodbye, My Son*, right?"

"The whole edition?"

"Five hundred copies. They pulped the rest. I've been selling them on Amazon. Or, not selling them. Four sales so far. Nobody wants to think about the problem until there's another mass shooting."

"Then they run around like chickens with their heads cut off."

"Precisely. And because they don't have heads, they forget there's a problem. Until the next time. It's awful."

"You're swimming against the tide, Joe. Nobody wants to eliminate gun violence. It's the best reality show going."

"Pretty cynical attitude, Andy boy"

"All this talk about the Gun Culture. People never seem to realize there's a Gun Control Culture too. The fact is, we've got these two herds of fanatics, each defining itself by its opposition to the other. If we took the guns away the whole thing would fall apart."

"That's just silly."

"Oh?"

"We've already got hundreds of millions of guns floating around this country. If we tried to take them away, we'd have another Civil War on our hands. The sensible thing would be to register and insure them, like cars. Force people to take responsibility for them."

"You'd have a tough time selling that one, Joe.

Registration is the first slip on the slope to confiscation. I could make it a rap if you like."

"Spoiled brats, that's what they are. Whiny drama queens prancing around in camo, waving scary guns. Everybody has to compromise in life, and they refuse to compromise. What you wind up with is 40,000 dead people a year, and madmen roaming the country with assault rifles and giant ammo clips."

Andy gave me a long look. "They're not called clips, Joe. They're never called clips. They're magazines. Mags for short. That's the real problem. You don't know anything about what you're condemning."

"Those years writing my book. You call that knowing nothing?"

"All due respect. You know statistics and you know slogans. You know nothing about guns and you know nothing about gun people, except that you hate them. The guns and the people both."

"Why shouldn't I? Look at all they've done for me."

"This isn't about you, Joe. I'm talking about the Gun Control Culture. You all claim the issue is guns, but it's way beyond that. It's class warfare."

"It is?"

"People with resources, Joe. People who can afford to be socially conscious. Liberal people who look down on... Look at the folks in this restaurant. Calorie junkies. I don't like the way they talk, look, or behave. That's the way gun people look to people who weren't raised around guns. People who know absolutely nothing about guns except that guns are bad. And how do the gun people react to that? They buy more guns to shove up those snotty liberal's... you know. How can you even talk about the issue if you don't know what it is? If all you know is *No*?"

Driving home with the mad whaling captain's journal on the seat beside me, Andy's words hung around my neck like the albatross. I'd always been aware that I was different from other kids. Scarred as a child by dark pangs of alterity, I wanted nothing more than to be like everyone else. A regular fellow. Maybe each of the ruddy-faced, snot-nosed boys I played baseball with at recess felt the same way. I have no idea.

But I do believe that inextinguishable longing was the reason Andy's argument had such a profound effect on me. Despite my college-honed literary proclivities I never identified as an elitist intellectual, and I certainly didn't want to be one of those liberals of whom Andy spoke—people who knew nothing about guns except that guns were bad. As I drove eastward on the Mass Pike that fine Indian Summer evening, an epiphany overtook me. I might as well have been run over by an 18-wheeler.

Said epiphany was as follows:

In order to properly address the problem of gun violence in America I—and everyone else who's similarly committed—needs to know as much about the issue as possible. Not just the slogans and ideas put forth by the people with whom we already agree, but everything. *Everything.* That simple observation, sprung on me by a book-gypsy, might just be the pivot on which my entire story turns.

Turns before me in the void even now. And I bear witness, almost as if I were praying.

From that fertile, fervid, Cracker Barrel moment, it became incumbent upon me to pursue the totality of the problem of gun violence in America, to gobble it whole, as earnestly as my fellow diners gobbled their Country Fried Steak and Chicken N' Dumplin' dinners. I needed to *consume* the problem in order to embody its solution.

The long and the short of it is that I bought a gun.

Sometimes you hear a noise—a faint humming, a thumping, or the sound of a distant machine—and you look about, trying to identify its source. Then in the midst of doing something else you realize the sound is still there and you become curious about it again and walk around the room putting your ear to the wall. Is there a leak in a pipe? Is the refrigerator about to die? Then you realize the sound is generated by the vast, shadowy apparatus of your life. It is the sound you were born with and are hardly ever attentive enough to hear.

I bought a gun because I'd had an argument with the wrong guy. Not to shoot him with, but because he was right. Anyway, I didn't just run out and buy one. I thought about it for a long time in the wake of my dinnertime argument with Andy, which was less an argument than an epiphany.

Sadly, this led to the dissolution of my marriage. A most painful sacrifice! Had I not been so intent upon solving the problem of gun violence, I might have headed off the situation with Bethany and her lover.

One morning, not long after my momentous conversation with Andy Willets, I woke from a dream so intense that I could not tell, at first, where I was, except that part of me was still stuck in the dream. In the dream I'm leaving my house, headed across the street to the Book Palace. The sky is a gray dome with a brilliant streak of red in the east. The air is pink. As I descend the porch steps, I see that my front walk is scattered with boughs of balsam fir. I reach the end of the walkway and look out on the road and it, too, is covered with Christmas greens, up and down as far as I can see. They cover the parking lot and the lawn in front of the Book Palace. Deep, fragrant greens in the luminous dawn.

And I think, *Someone has come and covered our town with Christmas greens. What a marvelous thing to do!* I am overwhelmed by the kindness of that act, the anonymous goodness someone has bestowed upon us all.

It was one of the loveliest moments of my life, and it happened in a dream. But what does it matter where it happened? That's what I was thinking when I woke, though I had no idea how long I'd slept since that dream moment. I just lay there, feeling myself coming back into the world, fully aware of its wickedness, and yet at peace.

That was when I heard the sound that was my life—far away at first but increasing in volume. I rode it back into my body.

Bethany lay beside me, making happy sleep-snortles as she breathed. I rose quietly so as not to wake her, dressed, got in the car and drove west, breakfasting and performing my morning ablutions in a MacDonald's en route, to the dumpy Lion's Club function hall on the outskirts of an old mill town an hour away. I was about to make the first of what would ultimately be a series of gun show visits, often appended to my book-buying excursions through gun-friendly states. I'd been thinking about this first one all week and, as I paid my $5 admission to the smiling lady at the card table in the lobby, I noticed that the sound was still there, idling like a car out front. I was all attention now.

Months of gun shows, until they all became one—the way all the bars become a single bar in a drunken evening's pub crawl. A long run of beards and bellies that would not have been out of place in a Cracker Barrel. A surprising number of women. Well, not really many women. A few wives, girlfriends, daughters, but any number in that context would have surprised me. Not as many guns as I'd expected, though their variety was at first bewildering. And lots of junk—leather belts and holsters, knives, flashlights, Tazers, WW II Nazi memorabilia, used books, ammo in tatty boxes that had been lugged from show to show, scopes, bayonets, pieces of hardware for assault rifles (inevitably camo, desert sand, or matte black finish), clever bumper stickers such as "If guns are outlawed, only outlaws will have guns," or the perennial "Guns don't kill people, people kill people."

Speaking of which, those people working the show (whose peoplehood, in my view, qualified them as potential killers), seemed friendly enough; generally aggrieved, but not overtly angry, though a few talked about "freedom" in a way that made the word sound like a high explosive. In general, it was possible to pick up the vibe (I picked up the vibe) of people who were interested in guns not as death machines but in the same way one might be fascinated with model trains.

I did a great deal of preliminary research. I had lengthy technical conversations with the people at those gun shows. I read gun magazines and spent hours on YouTube watching guys take guns apart and put them back together and blast the bejeesus out of bottles full of colored water, and cardboard silhouettes of people, and targets with cartoon Muslim faces on them. I watched women shoot, and men and boys and girls shoot. I read and watched consumer reviews of various guns, and I watched instructional videos about the many ways in which the AR platform might be configured.

And I have to admit, Andy's assessment had been correct. I did not care for these people and their guns. I found them aesthetically displeasing. But I stuck with it and eventually I got used to the leering hicks, the tight-minded old farts, the tattooed thugs, the sad, scrawny, wannabe soldiers of fortune. Maybe I just stopped seeing them, and started seeing the guns. After that it became somewhat more interesting to watch, for example, the YouTube video of the lady in Texas with the pink Beretta, or the guy shoulder-bumping his AR so that it fired as if it were on full auto.

I signed up for the gun course at the Sportsman's Club. Ninety-five dollars bought me a morning of instruction followed by a few minutes of wrapping my hands around cold steel (polymer, actually) and firing single and double action pistols. This was an exciting moment for me, another pivot. And it was marked by an unusual occurrence. A talismanic event.

When you fire a semi-automatic pistol, each spent cartridge is ejected as the next bullet loads, and the expended casing flies a few feet in an unpredictable direction. That's why we wear safety glasses on the range, and why baseball caps are suggested. Somehow, during the bang bang part of my training session, with all that brass flying around, an empty casing—perhaps from the pistol of the student next to me—found its way into the right pocket of the Carhartt vest I'd worn to class. I didn't discover it until that afternoon, when I put my hand in the pocket and felt an unidentified object, which I pulled out and identified as an expended .22 shell. I put it back in my pocket, and every time I stuck my hand in, I rolled the little brass cylinder around in my fingers. This produced an excitement from a place I could not identify. Put my finger on, you might say.

When the weather warmed I went down to Smitty's Gun Shop and saw, in a glass case, a pistol I recognized.

It was a Ruger LC9s, a small 9-millimeter handgun that had gotten good reviews in the gun magazines. It was a modest little thing, one of the early entrants in the craze for concealable pistols. I took a calming breath and told the guy behind the counter that I'd hunted as a kid, but hadn't done any shooting since my days in the military. Could he show me how this gun worked?

He could, and in short order I found myself engaged in a distinctly American rite of passage. The salesman gave me a form on which I entered my personal information and checked "no" next to each of a number of questions intended to ascertain my fitness to own a gun. Was I a drug addict? Had I ever been "adjudicated as a mental defective?" I could have been as crazy as the kid who thought God was commanding him to kill my son, but if my criminal record was clean and if I kept a straight face, the purchase would go forward.

The salesman took my paperwork into the back room, where he ran my information through the National Instant Criminal Background Check System. Fifteen minutes and a few hundred dollars later, I was an official gun owner.

Now I knew precisely the word for the feeling that shell casing gave me every time I felt for it in my vest pocket. The word was "transgressive" and the effect was steroidal. I was the father of a gun-murdered child and I had taken a gun course and gotten a gun license and purchased a gun. I wasn't supposed to be doing this, but I was doing it anyway, and now there was a new chapter in my story, a new turn. Not only was I the father of a gun-murdered child, I was also the knowledgeable, gun-owning father of a gun-murdered child. Never again would I call a magazine a clip.

One other thing I realized as the power of my discovery surged through me—when you walk down the street knowing you are lethal, there can be no such thing as a "modest" gun.

Then those ten people got slaughtered in that night club in Newark, New Jersey. That was the one where the shooters called 911 and praised Allah while the massacre was going on. You could hear the shots and screams. As you may recall, the country went into a tailspin of terror, terrified of terrorists. No one was safe. Then they caught one of the three shooters and it turned out the whole thing had been part of a drug war. It all seemed better then, which is shameful.

I'd started taking shooting lessons from a guy recommended by the salesman at Smitty's. He was a retired ATF agent and a part-time consultant for one of the higher-quality gun manufacturers. His approach was businesslike, matter-of-fact, and respectful. Guns as model trains that can kill. I liked him and, as my military training came back to me, I found that I liked the Zen of the whole thing—the stance, the breathing, the focus, the squeeze—getting my little Ruger to do my bidding without bidding. Then the acknowledgment from the pistol, which seemed almost jovial once I got used to it. The breath, the flash, and pow! An affirmative punch back at me. *There, now. Look what we've done!*

Anyhow, when I went back for my third lesson I mentioned the night club shooting and he said, "It scares the crap out of me."

"Really?" I was surprised that someone like him would have gotten the bug.

"Gun sales skyrocket every time these shootings happen, but this one pushed them through the roof. People run out and buy a gun and not one in twenty of them will take the trouble to learn how to use it. Now when I go to the mall, I get the creeps. All those guns in pockets and purses. All those people with guns they don't know how to shoot."

Freedman was the next one to make my hit parade.

I had a friend in a nearby town who let me shoot on his woodlot, but when he put the property up for sale I began frequenting the outdoor range at the Sportsman's Club. During one of my first visits, I noticed that several of my fellow shooters used targets with faces printed on them. Prominent Democrats and a Bin Ladenesque caricature were big favorites, but one guy was blasting away at the face of a black man in a do rag. I knew him slightly—the blaster, not the blastee—we'd been in a volleyball league together back in the day. I'd always considered him a harmless oaf, and his ugly display of racism astonished me. As we walked off the range I asked him, in the friendliest, most offhanded manner I could muster, if the face belonged to anyone in particular. He looked at me like I was crazy. "You been living under a rock, Joe? It's fucking Dellinger."

I squinted at the stack of unused targets as he was stuffing them back in his bag, and recognized the face of Jimmy Dellinger, the rookie quarterback who'd beaten the Patriots in last year's Super Bowl thanks to a widely disputed call on the final play of the game. I'd been so wrapped up in issues surrounding my personal growth that I'd failed to recognize Dellinger's smug puss. An embarrassing moment, but it inspired a therapeutic diversion.

It so happened that, while surfing the Internet a few days later, I came across an article in *The Guardian*—Europeans are obsessed with American gun violence—about Arthur Freedman, the man who ran the private equity firm that owned a number of gun companies, including the one that makes the Gaboon Viper, the especially fine gas-piston AR that killed the twenty-four in Ensenada, the eighteen in Atlanta, seven in St. Pete, and set the new record in the gun-slaughter Olympics—eighty-three men, women, and children at that festival on the island in Lake Champlain. According to the article, instead of dumping Viper Inc. after the Lake Champlain mess, Freedman doubled down on his investment, knowing sales would skyrocket in anticipation of a possible gun ban. A gun ban he knew would never happen, because he was spending millions to make sure it didn't. Mister Arthur Freedman was the perfect representative of the unseen forces of governance, perfectly loathsome, and perfect for what I had in mind, because he happened to look like a dyspeptic rat.

I photoshopped his rodent face onto an 11 x 17

sheet, laid the concentric circles over that, and made twenty copies on heavy paper. The next Saturday I set Freedman up on my stand and went for the beady eyes. It was heavenly. The Patriots fan was a couple of bays down from me, and when I was finished I futzed around with my gear until he stepped off the range.

"So who was that?" he asked.

"Arthur Freedman," I smiled. He was going to ask me who Freedman was, and I was going to tell him, sort of shove the identity up his ignorant, gun-loving... you know.

But he just said, "Oh," and went out to the parking lot.

This is hard.

I come across from the Book Palace one day and she's sitting there with her sob sisters, Brenda and Rachel. In the years since Ryan's death Brenda, Rachel, and Hallie have become Bethany's constant companions. She calls them her "Angels." God knows what they do together. Singer-songwriters sing softly in the background. There is tea, there are long walks. Some gaiety. Movies and books passed back and forth. *Goodbye, My Son* was greeted with smiling tears of approval, followed by hugs.

All very good. I send my smiling tears of approval back to those dear Angels, who are taking such good care of my poor, broken wife. I love the Angels. I enjoy making them laugh, which they are almost always ready to do, with me, at me—makes little difference. The laughter, Bethany's in with theirs, is nectar to me. I am fondest of Rachel, who is slender like Bethany, but dark haired, quick of eye, and bigger breasted. I fantasize three-ways, and am liberated in my fantasies by what I know to be their absurdity.

Hallie is the most attractive intellectually, but she never quite fits into my three-ways. Her sense of humor is dangerous, unpredictable. We'll be flirting along and then it'll break. I've said something or thought something or made some incorrect gesture, or *she's* thought something, and it's not funny anymore, and I am wrong. I could never get to the bottom of it.

Where is she, anyway?

Brenda is sandy haired, square faced, with just the faintest lisp at the end of her tongue. The sweetest person you can imagine. If I were back in the retail used book business she'd be at the counter waiting on customers. Unflappable.

Little is ever said about Ryan. These women do not inhabit Barbara Jackson's ghetto, where mention of her son Cooper brings him back from that pool of blood on the sidewalk. Was Barbara ever like Bethany, clinging to her sorrows, as if she thought that abandoning them would be to abandon her son? For years I thought Bethany just needed more time, but no. There would never be enough time for her.

Senator Perkins, my old political patron, explained it to me. I'd been selling him books about yachting, and he liked me, for whatever reason. One day he called me up, right out of the blue. It was the summer after Ryan had been killed. I was sitting in the Book Palace, waiting for Hank to show up, wondering if we'd ever sell another book, when the phone rang.

"We lost our daughter, you know, nearly twenty years ago now, in a cycling accident." He had a gently rumbling voice and a touchingly stilted, self-effacing manner of speaking. If you were over eighteen years of age he'd put "Mister" in front of your surname until you asked him to stop. I think it helped immensely in his political career. Not that he needed any help. He was born to that Senate seat.

"Yes, I know."

"You probably know that we helped create safe cycling lanes."

"Yes."

"We felt it was the least we could do. But for a long while before that I was unable to let go of my grief. We missed her so terribly, and I was afraid that if I got on with my life, I would be abandoning her somehow."

"Mmm..."

"Well, I just wanted you to know that I was wrong. It's been twenty years now and she's as close to us, as much in our hearts, as she ever was. And we've long since moved past that anguish, the grief I was so reluctant to give up... You don't have to get stuck there."

God, what a wonderful phone call! Senator Perkins died a couple of years ago, and his son took over the Senate seat. I told Bethany what the old man had told me, but she never got the point, never wanted to. She was going all the way down with Ryan.

Sitting there with Rachel and Brenda, as I was saying. I had long since transferred Senator Perkins's advice about not grieving for Ryan to not grieving for myself (my old life), then to not grieving the extinction of my courageous, dead-as-a-doornail memoir. I'd let all that go, and was feeling pretty good again, actually.

So, I walk into the kitchen, into my own house. No...

JANUARY 14
—BETHANY, SECOND TRY

One day I come across from the Book Palace and there are Brenda and Rachel sitting at the kitchen table in my house with Bethany. Hallie's gone off somewhere, or hasn't arrived yet, but they've left a chair for her. The conversation proceeds in murmurs, quiet and slow, same as it ever was, same as it ever was. But all of a sudden, I'm feeling a low-voltage hum of sexual energy.

Then I'm sick with it.

Then the world stops. Or, I stop. Or, the *moment* stops without warning—that's more like it—and all the trillion moments behind slam into it. Slam into me. The years since Ryan's death come together and pile up like a train wreck. Bethany and Hallie are lovers. They're sleeping together. They're fucking however women fuck.

The instant I see this I see that I've known it, at some level, for years. All the time I was out there giving my speeches and trying to push my book, all those years of telling myself I was providing for my family (whatever "family" represented in my inflamed imagination), all the gun research field trips and hundreds of hours of firearm acculturation (in the name of gun violence prevention advocacy!), all that time I convinced myself it was okay because the Angels were taking care of her—and they *were* taking care of her, and Brenda and Rachel were a couple, too—I must have known what was going on with them. The first day they walked in together from Hallie's book group I must have known. I knew. I know I knew. I felt like an idiot.

However, my immediate reaction to this untoward situation had nothing to do with the time I'd spent studying guns and advocating against gun violence. At that moment it had everything to do with the monumental discomfort I felt dwelling in the house that used to be Ryan's house, in Bethany's overflowing sadness bin, in the nexus of Parkinghamish disgust at my failures as a husband and a breadwinner, in that cave of sacred agony, guarded by Angels, the place of our suffering. The palace of our suffering.

The sad thing is, aside from that discomfort, and a vague curiosity about what they actually *did* together, I couldn't locate my feelings about Bethany's abandonment of me. What I felt was... nothing. A den of death-crazed lezzies? Oh well.

The Angels saw a storm coming and flew away. Bethany flushed red, and denied, denied, denied.

"Joe, what is *wrong* with you?"

"What's wrong with *me*? I've been out there working my ass off while you loll around here with your, your... whatever she is."

"I can't believe you could even imagine..."

"I'm not going to do this anymore. It's humiliating."

"That damned gun, Joe. This whole crazy trip of yours..."

"Don't give me that crap. My research has nothing to do with you and your girlfriend."

"How can you say that?" Hot breath. Her fury right up against my own. "All I ever hear about anymore is guns. Can you imagine how that makes me feel? Our son was killed by a gun, in case you've forgotten. But no. You've gone nuts with this thing. You know that, don't you? Coo-coo. Gaga. Off your trolley." All her years of sweet sorrow fermenting into toxic brew. I couldn't breathe its fumes.

"I've FORGOTTEN?"

Her eyes taunted me. I pushed back. One of the kitchen chairs caught her behind the knees and she fell, then was back up as quickly as if she'd bounced. Cocked like a mongoose, striking at me. "How dare you!"

I turned away She got my ear. I pushed again. She screamed. I put my hand to the side of my head. I was bleeding. She'd cut me.

I hardly need tell you it was a long summer. We avoided one another for the duration, which turned out to be easy. We needed to not speak while we read the writing on the wall.

September's cooler weather calmed us. The Angels fluttered back to the edge of the feeder. Bethany left a note about the oil burner. As I was crossing the street from the Book Palace, I saw her getting into her car. I shouted to her, "I'll wait for the furnace guy. You go ahead and do what you need to." And we were talking again. But never, ever, about that night.

Just round and round it, and back and forth and up and down. She turned the whole thing upside down on me. I doubted myself. I doubted her. She was my enemy. I was my own worst enemy. The three of them were against me, had me cut off at every turn. It was all my fault. I began experiencing petit mal seizures of nutty, blinding rage.

Months of tedious, weepy conversations. At some point Hallie showed up and refused to stop showing up until we got this thing straight. We had too much invested in one another, she said, to throw it away. ("On some cockamamie fantasy of yours" was left unsaid.) The three of us. The two of us. The five of us.

The day Bethany moved out was saturated with

compassion. She'd rented an apartment on Lewis Street, about a mile from Hallie's.

"I can't do this anymore," she told me, stealing my line. "We're keeping the house, Joe. You and me. I'll leave my things here, most of them, and we won't tell my folks, so..."

So the Parkingham dole would continue. I told her, "I don't want the house."

"You don't have to want it. You don't even have to live here." Her first flash of anger since that awful night, curiously clear and strong. I could sense that Hallie was good for her. "We're going to keep the house just the way it is, and we'll do holidays with my mom, and when she comes to visit, it will be like always. Maybe sometimes you'll be on the road. Do you understand what I'm saying?"

"Yes." We hadn't had sex in years. It was difficult after Ryan died. Too fraught. Then we just quit. I quit.

"You should see someone, Joe."

"A little late for marriage counseling, isn't it?"

"I don't mean that kind."

She was staring at me, velvety brown pools to drown in. I began to weep.

"You're not impotent, Joe. You're depressed."

Bethany continued her denials, kept trying to switch it onto my gun violence work. Then she added a note. If we'd truly been interested in maintaining our relationship, she would have felt guilty about moving out. But since I was the one who'd lost interest in her (although she never put it quite that baldly) she could care about me and be concerned for me without those feelings being tainted by guilt. Furthermore, since she knew, by my own insistence, that I was constitutionally incapable of guilt, we should be able to dispense with guilt altogether and get on with what she referred to as a more "normal" relationship.

The poor thing sounded as if she were reading from a script. Bethany didn't believe in science or in the scientific method. Her evidence was sensual, anecdotal, and her conclusions were intuitive leaps. This carefully reasoned argument bore the mark of another maker. And I had a pretty good idea who that maker was.

Hallie sat me down one night and poured us both a stiff one. "We're not going to get through this unless we do it together."

"Yeah." Bossy bitch.

"I mean we've got to get Bethany through this."

"Through what, exactly?"

"She doesn't know what she wants, Joe. You're hurt, sure. But you can see where she's at. You've always been so good at that. I know you care for her. Can't you see what's going on?"

"What's going on?"

"She has no idea. She doesn't know what she wants. She needs comfort, and she needs shelter. But what she really needs is to find her way back into the world. For now, we have to be the world for her. You and I, and everyone who cares for her. We have to make her strong again. She needs you, Joe. She needs all of us."

More Jack. More talks. More tea. More tears. I could see what they were up to, and I resented it. On the other hand, they were feeding me and keeping me company. I wasn't the only one who needed to survive this.

As you may have gathered from my observations on this matter, I have serious problems with the language that trails in the wake of gun violence. December 15th was the anniversary of Ryan's murder, though I detest the misuse of that word. Anniversaries are supposed to be occasions of celebration. The date of Ryan's death did not call for a celebration. He'd been murdered, not "taken" or "lost." He'd never been in "the wrong place." And what kind of halfwit would issue a "trigger warning" to a traumatized victim of gun violence? When gun meets human there is hardly ever a good outcome. Every term relating to that meeting has been so over-used, so taken-in-vain and abused, that it deserves to be put in ironic quotation marks. Believe me, once it's happened to you, your entire life might be placed inside inverted commas, so insubstantial, so unlike whatever you thought it might have been, has a gun rendered it.

By the afternoon of December 15th our relationship had improved to the point that I was able to pick Bethany up and drive with her to the cemetery, where we set up a little Christmas tree over Ryan's grave. This was a ritual we performed every year and, our disrupted relationship notwithstanding, it was not, nor had it ever been, the bitter occasion you might imagine. It was simply the last and only thing we could still do together, as a family, including Ryan. And it was sweet—the little tree, the memories. Bethany's monumental sadness had a part in it, sure, and my sadness for her and for Ryan and for myself. But during those few minutes at Ryan's grave, stringing the string of glittery snowflakes and angels round and round the baby tree, our sorrows seemed no more than a cloud bank on the horizon.

We stopped off at Hallie's when we were done. They'd have their tea, of course, but it was cocktail hour for me and the girls kept a bottle of Jack in the pantry.

As we walked into the kitchen, Hallie looked up from her phone. She was weeping.

"You won't believe this," she said.

The massacre at John Calhoun Junior College, with all its eerie similarities—the gun smuggled onto campus, the warning that came too late, the thirty-round magazines that, this time, did not fail. Five years to the day after the Brier Hill College shootings. Our hearts flew to where those thirty-three families were. We knew what they'd be living through in the days and years to come.

I wrote an op-ed, a short, powerful piece playing on the coincidence of those five years, and all that had happened and had not happened in that span. My man Daniel, down at Meyer Creative, called in a favor, and a few days later, while politicians across America were still calling for moments of silence, my piece appeared in the *New York Times*. "Our children are paying with their lives for a so-called freedom their elders enjoy," I told the world. Surely people would hear me this time!

They did not.

El Ninos of hot air issued from Capitol Hill but the cowardly Senate, even in the wake of thirty-three slaughtered teens, failed to pass even the most watered-down version of a gun bill. The whole disgusting fiasco convinced me that the JCJC shootings were just the latest in a long series of important issues that men had screwed up.

Because it wasn't white male politicians, African Americans, gay people, ghetto dwellers, or disabled vets who most resolutely demanded change. The only demographic consistently in favor of stronger gun laws—across the board, transcending party affiliation and gun ownership—was women. And what could be more antithetical to gun violence than family, than nurturing, than love? Not to be sexist about it, or to be quite sexist about it, this was feminine territory.

I worked that theme into an op-ed called "My Ted Talk is Pink." It was a positive piece, and I thought I'd done a good job of stressing the importance of women in the future of the gun violence prevention movement. But Daniel couldn't sell it. *Cosmo*, *Vogue*, and *Huffington* weren't interested. Nobody was interested, not even the local paper. The grisly coincidence that two school shootings could happen on the same day five years apart was interesting to people, nothing else.

Robots, hurry up!

It was Rachel, of all people, who told me about Americans Together. Help arrives, unbidden, from every quarter.

One night, fairly well along in our process, Bethany, Hallie, and I decided to go down to Sherm's House of Pain for a drink. The place had been a hangout for our crowd back in the day, but Bethany and I hadn't been there since Ryan died. I could imagine what it would be like to walk into Sherm's. The music and conversation would stop, and everyone would turn and stare at us, and we'd, I don't know, we'd incinerate or something. All at once, and once again, sitting in the front seat of Hallie's Subaru, I was right up against that infinitely elastic but utterly impermeable membrane between then and now.

I'd encountered it many times in the course of writing *Goodbye, My Son*, as I revisited the life Bethany and Ryan and I had lived together. I'd be walking down a street where we once pushed the stroller. Or maybe I'd be pacing the campus of Brier Hill College re-enacting the night of the crime, and suddenly I'd sense the past there in front of me, configured identically to the moment I was in, but right on the other side of it. I'd feel so strongly that if I kept going, just another step in that direction, I'd get there, and Ryan would be back as he so often is in my dreams, and our old life, the one that withered and died the night of the fatal phone call from Brier Hill, would be restored. I'd be back in a corner of it, maybe the field behind Ryan's dorm, and from there I'd go to his room and hug him and know his familiar smell once again, and we'd joke and get in the car and drive home to Bethany for summer vacation, and his job flipping burgers, his friends spilling out of our house.

Just exactly that sensation, the instant of stepping through the door at Sherm's for the first time in years. One more step. Bethany and I would go home after a while and catch the end of "Saturday Night Live," then crawl to bed, having fallen asleep in front of the TV and, half awake, smiling asleep, listen to Ryan sneaking in with Simone and the gang, trying to be quiet, then forgetting to be quiet. Then I'd come down in my underwear and tell them to shut the hell up and they'd squeal in terror. It was a game we played. God, every detail.

How could it be so present and so inaccessible? How could there be so much Ryan and no Ryan at all? The door closed behind us and the din in Sherm's went on unabated. Hallie spotted Rachel sitting at a table with some people I didn't know, and we claimed the adjacent table. I was closest to Rachel and she began shouting at me—the band was loud enough that you had to shout, but not so loud that you couldn't be heard at all. She asked me if I knew about Americans Together.

"Americans?" I thought she was talking about the band.

"It's like Mothers Against Drunk Driving except it's gun control. I heard about them on NPR. Walter says they've got a local chapter."

I'd asked the girls to read "My Ted Talk is Pink" and, predictably, they thought it was wonderful. Not only did they bestow teary hugs, they started forwarding links on Facebook that took me to petition drives, news stories about horrific shootings, and op-ed pieces suggesting new solutions for gun violence. Their motherly efforts to direct my gun thing were a little embarrassing, a little annoying, mostly sweet.

However, despite her fetching black tanktop under open denim work shirt, I couldn't focus on Rachel or what she was saying to me that night. I was stuck on the wrong side of the membrane, looking in at a life I'd lost. When they dropped me off after our drink at Sherm's,

I didn't go inside our empty house. I went across the street and slept on the cot in the back room of the Book Palace. The whole place smelled of Hank, kind of a wet dog smell, noticeable but not unfriendly.

A morning or two later I had to go downtown to get some money. Driving along Middle Street I saw a parking space in front of the Unitarian Universalist Church. The parking meter thingie was still green so I parked and went in. I don't think I would have stopped if I hadn't found that parking spot. The universe lines things up around you just so. You don't have any choice, but you don't know you don't, so it doesn't matter. You think you do.

I could see what Bethany and her Angels liked about the soaring, dim space inside the church, though I'm not a churchgoer myself. It smelled of furniture polish, and dust, and seat cushions, and it was calm, and sad with the sadness of ages; calm with the sadness because sadness was the normal course of things. All the Saviors give their lives for us, and we muddle along in our benighted, human way, failing always to take advantage of the gift, and it's sad.

Walter, the minister, was a sweet guy. He'd been a frequent visitor in the days right after Ryan died. What I liked about his visits was that he'd never say much. He'd just sit there looking awkward and pained. After a while we'd have to start talking just to make him feel better. It worked every time.

I found him in the garden behind the church, raking leaves. He was a balding, spindly little fellow perpetually in a questioning mode. He suffered from depression, and every once in a while, he'd have to go away, but his parishioners supported him; he assumed the burden of their questions, and they loved him for that. He was also a walking social service referral agency. Suicide, addiction, domestic violence, you name it and he'd hook you up with someone who could help you. Maybe that was why they loved him. I told him what Rachel had told me about the gun control group, and he said he'd look into the matter.

A few days later Walter called and gave me the contact info for Mindy at Americans Together Against Gun Violence, also known as Americans Together. I sent her an email and she telephoned me the next day, which impressed me. She asked me if I felt comfortable sharing my story, a locution I would soon be using myself. It was crafted to acknowledge that we were having our conversation in a very different sort of place than the one in which normal discourse occurs; a safe place, but one of suffering and sympathy, not unlike the place of supreme sorrow colonized by Bethany and her

Angels or the vast uterine cave in which Walter went about his business.

I told her my story and asked if she'd read my book? She confessed that she had not heard of my book. However, she promised to obtain, and read, a copy "Today. As soon as we're finished here." She was reaching out to me on Walter's recommendation, she said, because Americans Together was in the process of creating a National Victim Alliance Network. Victims of gun violence, she told me, were at the heart of the Americans Together movement. We were the ones who had suffered the terrible consequences of weak gun laws, and they needed people like me, people who were not afraid to speak up, to reach out to other victims, to help them find the courage to share their stories, so that everyone could see the true cost of gun violence. Would I consider becoming a statewide coordinator in their new National Victim Alliance?

I'd been trying, virtually since the night of Ryan's murder, to get people to listen to my story. But to date my voice had been no more than a lonely howl. What Mindy was offering, if I heard her correctly, was a larger platform.

She had me at "National."

Soon I was deep in training for my role as statewide

representative of the National Victim Alliance Network, attending lengthy telephone conferences about best practices for influencing legislators, or struggling through web-based tutorials that were intended to teach me how to navigate the National Victim Database (they failed to do so)—aware, all the while, that the coexistence of this enterprise and my gun studies could be interpreted as a schizoid confusion of purpose. True to my mandate, I entertained that possibility and ultimately concluded (I knew it all along) that the two disparate endeavors were in perfect balance.

"This is awful." Vicky put her hand on my arm as she spoke, causing my endorphin machine to creak into action.

We'd met the day before, at National Victim Alliance Leader Orientation, in the Dolphin Room at the new Harborside Hotel in Boston. The hotel had cranked up the air conditioning and I noticed that the woman seated beside me was hugging herself, rubbing her biceps the way people do when they're cold. Short blond hair, bunny rabbit mouth, green eyes, modest breasts. Cute in a funny-looking but beguiling sort of way.

I leaned over and said, "You're cold. Would you like my shirt?"

"Off your back?""

"That one, yes."

"Not just now, no."

Intelligent, obviously. I thought, *I could fall in love with the way that silver chain hangs round her neck.*

Orientation was disorienting in the extreme. It was led by our facilitator, Danutia, an unpleasant woman who began by telling us about the important corporate and institutional clients she'd had in the past, and the excellent results she'd achieved. She was certain that, because we were so highly motivated, this training would produce similarly excellent results. She introduced her assistant, a black girl named Emeretta, and Emeretta stood up smiling, waved both hands to us the way campaigning politicians do, belted out an acapella version of "Amazing Grace," and sat back down. I wasn't sure what the purpose of that performance was, but it made me uneasy. She was blind.

Then Danutia went slowly, meticulously, in painful detail, over every hour of our schedule for the next two days. She did this, she explained, because people who are suffering from post-traumatic stress often feel disoriented. This was why, in our future work with victims of gun violence, we should do everything possible to insure there would be no surprises. It was, she said, an aspect of PTSD that many of us were familiar with.

I thought back over my career as a traumatized victim and decided I was familiar with disorientation. However, I could not recall instances of mood cycling or high anxiety to which she also referred. Sleeplessness was certainly a symptom I knew, as well as feelings of numbness—Bethany!—and irrational outbursts of anger. Though I took issue with the "irrational" part.

As far as I was concerned, I had plenty of damned good reasons to be angry. In any event, this listing and discussion of symptoms went on until heads were bobbing around the Dolphin Room. A sufficient number of symptoms had been identified to allow each of us to feel some ownership of post-traumatic stress. Danutia explained this was the reason why grounding and self care were so important. She asked us to rise from our folding chairs. We rose. She crossed her hands over her heart and instructed us to do the same.

"Now, close your eyes. Imagine green fields and blue skies. Take a deep breath, hold it... exhale. Again... A beautiful dawn. Dew on the lawn. Once more. Hold it. Exhale. And one last time. Now, eyes open. Shake it out!" And, just short of hyperventilation, or perhaps possessed by that dizzying state, she showed us what to do by wiggling her shoulders and meaty arms, an exercise we mimicked as best we could. Emeretta jumped up and sang a startling chorus of "Shake it Up, Baby," then sat back down beside Danutia. We began to talk confusedly among ourselves. Wasn't this fun? What was going on?

I turned again to the woman beside me and announced, "I do feel a little more relaxed."

She wore a look of absolute panic and a name tag that said *Vicky.*

Danutia began speaking but, in our newly relaxed or panicked states, we paid her little mind and continued talking among ourselves.

"Are you all right?"

"No... Yes."

As I was groping for some way to continue the conversation Danutia raised her hands over her head and clapped them together. Her palms made a solid crack. Like a gunshot, I thought, imagining us poor PTSD victims diving under our chairs. She shouted, "Clap once if you can hear me!"

A few people clapped.

She clapped twice. That brought us around. "Clap twice if you can hear me!" We clapped twice and shut up. Hands crossed over hearts again, deep breaths, this time with questions between the breaths.

Where am I? What is today? What is the date?

These questions oriented us in place and time, an important aspect of grounding, the end result of which was to get us in our bodies. I hadn't felt particularly out of my body, but apparently others had. Vicky had. Her name was Vicky Gimble and she was from Pettucket. I knew where Pettucket was! I'd been to McIver stadium to watch the PetSox play. She didn't live too far from the stadium. Well, no place in Pettucket was too far from the stadium, Pettucket being a small town. She'd never been to a baseball game at McIver, though she did watch an occasional Major League game on TV.

"Clap once if you can hear me!"

We stood in a circle in the front of the room and held hands. Danutia appointed a little gray-haired lady to squeeze the hand of the person to her left, and instructed each of us to pass the squeeze along as soon as we felt it. The gray-haired lady was to let us know when the squeeze got back to her, which she did after a surprisingly long interval, with a yelp. Then Danutia had us count off, one to six, and broke us into groups according to the number we'd called. These would be our teams for the next two days. Each team was assigned a facilitator from the staff. In this regard it had been a mistake to stand next to Vicky, though it was fun having her hand in mine.

During the ten-minute break before our first workshop, I wandered in a haze of exhaustion, clutching my can of Coke, looking at the people around me, some chatting in groups, some sitting alone, apparently as disoriented as I was. People of color, senior citizens, a few strapping young men, housewives, college kids—a human zoo of creatures with one terrible thing in common.

That commonality was what I thought about all through our team's first workshop, "Leaderful Networks," which was held in the Starfish Room. I thought about the many forms victimhood could take. Were there as many different kinds as there were people? And yet in that one horrible way they were all the same.

I thought about it at lunch in the Periwinkle Room, sitting at a table dominated by three black ladies who were, Lord be praised, trash talking one another, about their clothing mostly, accompanied by raucous laughter that was as sweet to my ears at that moment as the laughter of Bethany and her Angels. I looked around the room for Vicky, and saw her a couple of tables away, looking around the room for me. Our eyes met for an instant and we both continued panning around the room, as if that glance had been an accident, but it was not.

During a fifteen-minute postprandial session on self-care led by Danutia and accompanied by two songs from Emeretta, I thought about it. One of the songs was a bluesy version of the schmaltzy Seventies hit "Everything is Beautiful," which worked in exactly the way that clowns are sad. Or scary. And I thought about it through the second workshop, "Building and

Strengthening the Everyleader Community," which took place in the Marlin Room. And through the final session of the day, "All Indians are Chiefs," in the Dune Room.

Back in the Dolphin Room the teams gathered for a team-building exercise before dinner. Our team's facilitator was a coffee-colored girl—lady? She was so slight it was impossible to tell. Her name tag said *Aditi*. She addressed our team in a little cricket voice, "If there was one quality that would determine a person's suitability for Victim Alliance Coordinator, what would it be?" We were to discuss this with our team mates, formulate a group answer, and select a spokesperson to deliver it. Emeretta was the time keeper, somehow navigating the room, listening in on the discussions of one team after another, with a big smile on her pretty face, and those frightening, empty eyes. You got the feeling she was echo locating. And how did she keep track of time?

"Okay, people. Two minutes left. Wrap it up!"

The staff herded the teams back into circle formation, and each spokesperson in turn stepped forward from the group and announced the quality his or her team had selected, whereupon Danutia wrote the quality on a big whiteboard in the center of the circle, each quality written out in a different color marker. They were all excellent qualities.

At that moment I was overwhelmed by an unnamable but tremendous emotion, an oceanic feeling. I looked around the room at us standing in our groups, and my day-long meditation coalesced into the realization that we were not victims. The victims were dead. We were the survivors of those victims. And we were called survivors because we had survived. It felt similar to the sensation I'd had in the court room, the elation of ceasing to be a victim and becoming a reporter, but its resonance was enhanced by the number of people in this room who were contributing to the experience.

The feeling filled me and overflowed. I began to weep, not in a hysterical way, but heaving a bit with sobs. If the people around me noticed—how could they not?—they didn't make a big deal about it. The teammate on my left, a hulking motorcycle-gang-looking fellow with a pony tail, gave me a hug and thumped my back in a manly way. He smelled of Right Guard, an odor you rarely encounter these days. Then the emotion passed and I felt an enormous calm. He and I stood with our arms around each other's shoulders, comfortable as you please, listening to reports from the groups. We'd spent all day together, but I couldn't remember this fellow's name. I looked at his name tag. It said, *Hank*. Like my Hank. We all had the same name.

Twelve tables for dinner back in the Periwinkle Room, but the teams were encouraged to break up. I sought out Vicky, who now had a sweater with her. It was draped on the back of the chair beside her, and when she saw me, she removed it and gave the slightest gesture with her head and shoulders, like, *Over here, big boy.* I thought I could fall in love with the curve of her neck.

She told me, over our chicken picada, that Danutia and Emeretta creeped her out. She was put off by the prevalence of cant, psychobabble terms, and touchy feeliness, and she didn't know if she could last through the second day. I told her I didn't care much for Danutia, either. I suspected she was used to consulting for corporate groups and was tone deaf to victims. Vicky thought that was a possible explanation, but that it felt chemical to her. Chemical? Well, sort of like inverse pheromones. Repellent. Dislike at first sight, which made us laugh. I told her she wasn't allowed to quit, because if she quit, I'd quit too, and I didn't want to quit because I'd felt something powerful here. I told her what I'd experienced just a few minutes before, and she said, "Wow."

That was how, at the next morning's grounding exercises, after Emeretta had treated us to "I Can See Clearly Now," when Danutia, eyes closed and hands crossed over her heart, was intoning, "I am breathing in good energy. I am breathing out bad energy," I felt Vicky's hand on my arm. I opened my eyes and turned to see her looking at me. She said, "This is awful." But she was smiling.

The workshops, actually, turned out pretty well. We learned about such things as building networks, putting "the ask" on people, "tabling," and other forms of recruiting, advocating, and influencing. We learned about empowering victims and helping them share their stories, and we learned about how to transfer the personal information of story-sharing victims into the cloud-based National Victim Database, which Americans Together would use in its case against the proliferation of guns. We learned about constructive disagreements and how to keep a movement moving. Above all, we learned, it was our stories that would power the movement.

At the very end Danutia asked us to think back to the teams we'd been part of for the past two days. Eight to ten people was the ideal size for a group, and each of us now had the tools to form such groups, and to empower each person in that group to empower another eight or ten people, and so on into the world. That was how movements grew. "You can do this!" she assured us.

It also sounded to me like the recipe terrorists used for making sleeper cells but, no matter. As we were leaving, the staff handed out orange tee shirts bearing the handclasp logo of Americans Together and the slogan, "Together Against Gun Violence." On the back the shirts said, "National Victim Alliance—Whatever It Takes!" So, I said to myself, if sleeper cells were what it took...

Hank's old computer blew up a couple of days ago, and I had to order a new one. Maybe writing about my steamy affair with Vicky overheated it. Luckily, I save all my work in the cloud. All the records for Joseph Mooney Rare Books, Inc. are up there, too.

Nearly a week has passed since the last newspaper report on the murders and nothing further has appeared. Sometimes I can feel the cops out there, Feds probably, closing in on me, doing their best not to incite the millions upon millions of pissed-off survivors who are just waiting for an excuse to throw it all back in the faces of red-necked, white-faced American patriots. When I finish this memoir or confession or manifesto, or whatever it is, I'm going to send it to the *New York Times*, the *Washington Post*, and the *Wall Street Journal*. It'll be like dropping a match in a puddle of gasoline.

Image here of skiing down one of those perfect dead drops like you see on TV, the greatest rush in your skiing career, faster than you could imagine yourself going, in perfect form.

Several things stand out about my exhilarating ride down that slope.

Vicky was amazing, scary, inspirational. As a nine-year-old she'd watched her father shoot and kill her mother and then had heard, from the next room, the self-inflicted shot that ended his life. Can you imagine what something like that would do to a child? Me neither. Somehow, she survived, and now the incomprehension, hurt, and rage, hardened by decades, were coiled inside her. She was the fiercest person I'd ever met, and the most fragile. She took the train, that first time, from Pettucket to visit me. It was National Gun Violence Awareness Day, and Walter, with my help, had organized a vigil and a march from the UU Church to City Hall. Vicky and I bought ice cream cones at Dairy Train and I drove her around, showing her the sights.

She said, "Quilts, vigils, bells, moments of silence. Those NRA guys see us standing around with candles in our hands and they say, *Is that all you got?*"

And she said, "Sad bores me. People tell me how brave and strong I am. But I'm not brave or strong. I used all that up in the first five minutes. I'm just angry now. Angry that this happened to me, and angry that the world let it happen. Keeps letting it happen."

And she said, "Now they use my story to warn people about guns. But the stories just turn into news. Into entertainment. That's where they go to die, these supposedly important stories."

And she said, "The people at Americans Together. Do they ever think what happens to someone when all that's left of them is their story?"

She said these things and I was amazed. I thought she was going to cry, so I hugged her. But she didn't cry.

She said, "There's nothing left of them, that's what happens."

We kissed. We'd known it was going to go like this. Then she felt my erection and she gave me a hand job, right there in the car at the far end of the parking lot overlooking the river. Vigorous, lusty, cheerful, like in high school, or my dream of high school. I hadn't known it was going to go like *that*.

I thought I'd better change my pants before the vigil, so we went to the house. I told her my story as we drove—the part I hadn't told her before—about the failure of my book to find an audience, and about losing Bethany, and about Hallie and Rachel and Brenda. We sat at the kitchen table and I made us—what else?—cups of tea and went off to change. When I came back, she was sitting there, tea untouched, a distracted look about her. Was something wrong? She began to weep. What was the matter? She could not speak. The tears came in torrents. She was inconsolable. I was frightened. I kept asking, "What is it?"

"This house," she finally sobbed, as if her heart were breaking. "I can't be here. Please take me home." Maybe we should have gone to the Book Palace.

At that point I would have done anything for her, and I would have done anything to stop the crying, which was a different matter altogether. It was too bad about the vigil. The Angels would have been there, and I wanted them to see me with Vicky. But I certainly wasn't going to drag her down there in her present condition.

To my relief, her mood improved on the drive back to Pettucket. By the time we got to her place, a first-floor apartment in an ancient white clapboard house with many dormers, she was almost cheerful. I remember thinking, just for an instant, that I should have put a toothbrush in my pocket in case things went well. But before I could get any farther with that fantasy, she thanked me for the ride, hopped out of the car and went up the walkway without so much as turning around. I sat at the wheel watching her, wondering what I was supposed to do. She unlocked her front door, went in, and closed it behind her. On the drive home I tried to understand what had just happened, and failed.

I was washing the teacups when the phone rang. It was Vicky, calling to thank me for putting up with her and for driving her home. I assured her I was happy to help, and that being with her was very different than putting up with her.

"I like you," I told her. "I think you're funny and smart and (Say it, Joe!) sexy. I'm sorry things didn't work out today, but I'm not sure that means they never would."

"It wasn't you. I think I got overwhelmed inside your house. It's just hard for me to get close to people. And those things you told me about your family, I could feel them, and..."

"I understand."

"Well, I don't. I'm always the last to get the news. About myself, I mean." She sounded positively chipper. "Maybe sometime you could come down here and visit me. We could go to a ballgame."

"I'd like that."

We agreed that it would be worth a try, and hung up. The house seemed empty, cold. I turned the thermostat way up and poured myself a drink, thinking about my unexpected orgasm, trying and failing once again to get my mind around what had just happened. Always the last to get the news about myself. The phone rang again.

"It's me," Vicky said.

"I thought you'd never call." Things were in sync again, just like that.

"Shut up. There's an afternoon game this Sunday against Louisville. 1:05."

The game was boring. We left in the fifth inning. Was I interested in an early dinner? She knew a sweet little place on Federal Hill. I was interested, yes. We went back to her place for a drink and wound up having sex, wonderful sex, which, let's face it, we both knew very well might happen. I was neither impotent nor depressed.

That was the rhythm of our relationship. She was fucked up and fascinating. I'd approach, she'd pull away. Feral. She lived alone in an empty apartment. No paintings on the walls, almost no furniture. No friends that I ever heard about. Somebody must've been taking care of her, but we never talked about that. She was an adjunct English professor at CTCRI, whatever that was, and a serious reader, which turned out to be an unexpected boon for us. She gave me that marvelous book about flies by Frederik Sjoberg. I turned her on to James M. Cain, whom she'd never read. She devoured *Mildred Pierce* and told me it was the Great American Novel. Right under our noses, all this time.

Then blackness would sweep over us. There was no predicting the frequency of those events, but it was easy to see one approach. Sudden removal. Silence. Tears. I learned pretty quickly to clear out when I saw one coming, to spare her the additional heartache of throwing me out, of reviling me, of accusing me of things I couldn't possibly have done. It sounds uncaring, I know. But she needed to crawl into a hole until she got better. I'd withdraw and eventually she'd approach. It was always best right then, the first little while she was back.

I gave her *The Raymond Chandler Omnibus*, and she took up the endearing affectation of talking in hard-boiled fashion. At the breakfast table, for instance, sun streaming through her kitchen window, "Hey buddy, want another cuppa Joe?" Nipples outlined beneath her tee shirt. All I wanted was to fuck her and fuck her and fuck her. I wanted to love her. I wanted to be at that table forever, light filling the empty room, with her cracking wise out the corner of her mouth.

Let it be known that I tried my hardest to apply everything Danutia and the others had taught me, I really did. But my efforts to recruit victims into the National Victim Alliance met with little success. Some people promised to call back, but never did. Others allowed me to coax information out of them which I attempted, with mixed results, to feed into the ravenous National Victim Database. But none of those conversations ever went anywhere. People who'd talked to me once never picked the phone up when I called them back. At the end of the day not many survivors were interested in joining a National Survivor Alliance Network of similarly afflicted freaks.

At the end of the day, it was dark and I was moving across a battlefield. Cries of agony rose up all around me.

I spent much of the afternoon today wondering if I should include in these recollections a troubling episode that took place toward the end of my abortive career with Americans Together. It was strange in a way that, even now, makes me feel strange; I am disturbed by the wild thoughts and ideas it provokes. However, it did provide, if not a pivotal moment, at least another advance in my personal development. So I will record it here as faithfully as I can.

***

Thanks to my hard-boiled girlfriend things were going along pretty well, almost as if I'd struck a truce with whatever was raging inside me. Then a fellow named Cliff called from Americans Together.

The Texas State Legislature was about to pass a bill requiring the presence of at least two armed students in every college classroom, and Americans Together was lobbying hard to stop it. They wanted to bring some parents of children who'd been killed in campus shootings down there to talk to the politicians, to try to get them to understand what a bad idea student-owned guns on campus would be. I asked Cliff if he'd read my book. He said he had not, but that he was looking forward to reading it. Could I spare a couple of days to help them out?

Thus I found myself, rather too early one morning, at a breakfast buffet in the Sheraton Austin Hotel in Austin, Texas, with Jerry, our handler from Americans Together, and Thomas, a young man who had survived a school shooting, and with Patti and Robert—two other parents of school-murdered children. The big surprise was Emeretta who, it turned out, had been one of the seventeen students who'd survived (twelve killed) the infamous North Slope College shooting.

In that uncanny way of hers, Emeretta recognized my voice, one among the hundred she'd heard in the confusion of our training a year before.

"Hi, mister Mooney."

"It's Joe, please." I squeezed her hand. "I thought you worked for Danutia."

"No, she was just a consultant. I'm staff. I interned for Brady first, then got a real job with Americans Together. They're helping me with school. I've already got my MSW and now I'm working toward my LCSW."

I cocked my head in a quizzical manner, which she could not possibly have seen, but must have felt.

"Licensed Clinical Social Worker," she explained.

"Wow! When do you sleep?"

"In class. But they can't tell."

She chuckled, pleased with her bad girl blind joke, and I thought, *I could fall in love with that laugh.*

Somehow these Texas lawmakers had conflated the Second Amendment and the "one nation, under God" concept to mean that every American had a God-given right to walk around with a gun. In fact, concealed carry laws *already on the books* in Texas made it quite legal to be on a state college campus with a concealed firearm. It was just that, when you went into a classroom or into your dorm, you had to put the gun back in your pickup truck. The legislators aimed to repair that little inconsistency this time around.

Our handler took us to a series of crowded office ante-rooms, where weary staffers awaited us. Didn't we understand, their looks seemed to say, that we were only one among dozens of this day's supplicants, every one of them as convinced of their cause as we must be of ours, whatever it was? Whereupon we would tell them *exactly* what it was, gaining their attention for an uncomfortable few minutes. Every one of them, staffers and pols alike, when they realized who we were, put on the solemn mask and intoned, "I'm so sorry for your loss/grief/pain"—whatever word they could find to fit that desperate slot.

And we'd smile sadly and acknowledge their acknowledgment of our agonies, and launch gravely into our set pieces about the consequences of letting young adults with still-developing brains walk around a college campus carrying concealed firearms.

But what we were thinking as we spoke was something along the lines of, *Sorry? You're so fucking SORRY? Well, we don't want your "sorry." If you're so sorry, why don't you DO something about it?—something besides putting more guns in places they don't belong. Otherwise, you can shove your "sorry" up your fat, white, middle-aged...*

Or, *How much have you so-called Christians forgotten when you forget that God oversees your every breath? How far have you sunk when you can't trust in Him to see you safely across the street?*

Or, *You boys down here sure got some serious dick-size issues.*

Or maybe Emeretta, our sightless songbird, might have sung, *Sadness beyond sadness. I feel a sadness for your fear, your rage, your vanity. I feel a sadness for all the things you think you must protect, foremost of which is your ignorance. I feel a sadness for all you think you've lost, and a sadness for all you truly have lost. Guns kill. That's what they do. Guns rend, puncture, tear, destroy. I feel more sadness for you than I could ever express.*

Then, as if it had been nothing more substantial than a dream, our foray into Texas politics was over, and we were having beers at the airport, awaiting our flights home. Except Emeretta was having water because she didn't drink. Except that wasn't what *really* happened on my visit to Austin. By which I simply mean that something more important occurred the night before I left.

Following my State House labors I went down to 6th Street for a solitary meal of ribs and red beans, after which I stood on the corner getting my bearings and letting the ribs settle. I turned east toward the music for which that district was so well known but then, as unerringly as a compass needle, I spun around northward, toward the State House dome. The sun was just going down. The sky was deep blue overhead, orange and pink along its western edge, and darker to the east. Against the blue were discrete puffs of cumulus clouds, tinted pink, the kind of clouds you might see on a summer evening and note without remarking on them other than to think, *What a lovely evening!* which I thought to myself, staring contentedly at the dome and the sky and the clouds.

Then I noticed that these clouds were behaving in a most unusual manner as they moved across the blue from west to east. Their leading edges, the cottony wisps that looked like islands, death's heads, question marks, whales, or any of these, or all of them as I watched, these edges seemed to be curling beneath the denser mass of the cumulus puffs to which they were attached. The more I looked, in fact, the more it seemed the clouds themselves were tumbling, rolling their way across the Texas sky. I watched them tumble and thought how novel this was. Tumbling clouds! I became rapt or enraptured or wrapped up and moved as effortlessly as a cloud past the State House, up Guadalupe Street, and onto the campus of the University of Texas.

Looking at the buildings and trees and walkways in the gentle dusk, and at the students enjoying the evening, and at that tower, the iconic tower of the University of Texas, looming above, the very tip of it lit lurid red. I walked walkways and peered into windows, some of which were open, sending conversation, laughter, and music into the night. I passed students engrossed in their lives, engrossed in themselves, texting others similarly engrossed. I passed couples and groups, walking, holding hands, talking excitedly or quietly or not talking at all. Kids everywhere around me, and the tower above, Charles Whitman up there moving from slot to slot with his trusty Remington and his M1 carbine, aiming, taking this one, that one. One shot, one man, as he'd been trained to do during his unhappy hitch in the Marines. Bang! The fetus is murdered in her belly. The young husband, alarmed at he knows not what, says, "What's the matter, honey?" and Bang! He's dead, too.

That day, the day of the tower shooting, the first day of August 1966, I was just a kid. Mom and I watched the news on Huntley-Brinkley. Then the big article came out in *Time Magazine*. I studied it carefully, and thought how odd it was for someone to have done something like that. Bizarre, as if a mysterious object had dropped onto the earth from a distant planet. The incident became something of an obsession of mine.

I walked through the warm evening, college life throbbing around me, glancing up at the tower occasionally, thinking of Whitman's pudgy face, his crewcut, and the way he mourned his sanity, its loss, as if it were another of his departed loved ones. "I have been a victim of many unusual and irrational thoughts," he wrote. "It was after much thought that I decided to kill my wife, Kathy... I love her dearly and she has been as fine a wife to me as any man could ever hope to have. I cannot rationally pinpoint any specific reason for doing this."

I thought about all of that, walking back to the hotel, including the part about being terribly sick, and knowing it, and being unable to stop it, yet being able at the same time to form a plan and execute it so calmly, so methodically. And also, of course, I thought about bystanders getting their deer rifles out of their pickups and blazing away at the tower, running into the hardware store on Guadalupe Street for more ammo. I thought about the man bleeding on that plaza in the murderous sun. No one could get to him. Too much lead flying around.

That was what was going through my head the next day, as I sat in the airport bar with Emeretta and the others, and later at home, as the long month wore on. I thought about how the plantings and monuments are now arranged so that there are no unobstructed sight lines to shoot along from the tower, not that anyone is allowed up there anymore anyway, though you could still almost spit or certainly shoot from that lofty, red-tipped phallus of a structure down onto the State House, as close as it is to the campus. Or ejaculate, at the climax of your slaughter orgy, into the great, dim legislative chamber where, in the last hours of the last day of the legislative session, the wise men of Texas passed their revised Campus Carry bill into law, scheduled to take effect August 1st of the following year, which happened to be the anniversary (that word again!) of Charles Whitman's rampage.

Considering the matter overall, from the broadest possible perspective, as if I were aboard one of those tumbling clouds, it seemed that the passage of this dazzlingly stupid piece of legislation, the where and the when of it, the bland assumption of the politicians, their appalling lack of any sense of history, as well as their innocent failure to comprehend the ugly irony of what they had done, was uniquely, perfectly, grotesquely... well, *American*.

How odd are the things that happen in life! There's no coherence to them, and yet they fit. Americans Together and their squadrons of lawyers and lobbyists tug at the levers of power. Barbara Jackson and her people at the Church of Zion insert themselves into cycles of violence. My survivors and I share our stories in ritual tellings, lacerated as Indian Sun Dancers, flesh ritually pierced and flayed, trusting in our suffering to move the world. I begin to understand the ways in which the performative does indeed cause things to happen, is causing things to happen all around me—in a realm far beyond the political.

One day the National Victim Alliance Coordinator for the state of Illinois called. She said she'd met an interesting man who seemed eager to take part in our activities. He was a survivor of gun violence but he'd recently left Illinois and moved to my state, not far from where I lived. His name was Dennis Sykes and his younger brother had used a firearm to commit suicide. Dennis seemed to be doing okay, though one could never really be sure. Mostly, he was in that frame of mind where he needed to be doing something. She gave me his contact information and suggested I get in touch with him. Which I did immediately and with no little excitement.

We met at a Dunkin' Donuts. He was about my size, dressed in immaculate business casual. His features were so pleasingly regular that he could have been a business casual clothing model, although more J.C. Penny than Armani.

"I know this is always the hard part," he told me after we'd introduced ourselves and fumbled through the coffee buying ritual (he wouldn't let me pay). "So I'll get right to it. My brother Albert, who suffered from clinical depression, committed suicide with a shotgun on the family farm in southern Illinois three years ago last August. Both my parents had passed, so along with the trauma of his suicide, my younger brother and sister and I had to deal with the property, which had considerable value. It didn't go well. None of us were farmers, and there was a lot of pressure, financial and psychological, from local developers on one side and conservationists on the other. Things blew up between my brother and sister. I'd been living in the Bay Area at the time—I'd started a little tech company out there— but relations were so bad between them that I had to move back to Illinois."

This put his tech startup in limbo, so he sold it and invested the money with a partner, a fellow he'd known at Stanford, in a shipping logistics venture in the Chicago area. Unfortunately, the family situation turned out to be such a drain on his attention that the new business languished. The partner took the money and ran. "Antigua," he said, shaking his head sadly, "It's always Antigua." Dennis was forced into bankruptcy. Ultimately, it cost him his share of the farm.

His story became more complicated after that, a career path meandering through high-tech startups, a Christian ministry, a second wife, and the beginnings of his reinvention as a motivational speaker. His brother's tragic end had inspired him to want to make a difference in people's lives and, after what he'd been through with his siblings, to help people understand the basics of conflict resolution. "But, time," he said. "There's never enough time!"

Tables around us emptied and filled, emptied and filled. I'd consumed an everything bagel with veggie cream cheese and a medium coffee, regular sugar, extra cream. He'd barely touched his decaf. I had to pee.

A fascinating history, I decided, standing over the porcelain, told in a most evocative manner. I was drawn to him, and I knew he'd have this effect on others as well.

It was easy to picture Dennis as an Americans Together accomplice, the two of us going around like Jehovah's Witnesses—no, Butch Cassidy and the Sundance Kid. I returned to our booth, with some vague thought of exploring partnership possibilities. But Dennis saw me coming. As I took my seat he said, with pitch-perfect self-effacing irony, "But enough about me..."

I told him about Ryan, and the book, and my book business, and the marriage that had been a casualty of it all, and about Americans Together and the National Victim Alliance.

He said, "Tell me more about this book you wrote."

I told him.

He said, "And Ryan, what was he like?"

I told him.

He said, "Americans Together, the National Victim thing. I want to help. Tell me more about that."

He digested this information and then, more or less out of the blue, said to me, "You've got quite a way with people."

I told him he was pretty good himself.

He replied, mildly, that he knew he was. It was a trait that had made him successful in business and it was an aspect of his life that he was now determined to pursue. He asked me about our training. The work we were engaged in was complicated and delicate. How did they prepare us for it?

I told him about the several training sessions I'd attended, including the one at which I'd met Vicky, though I didn't mention her. I did tell him about the immense surge of emotion that had resulted from realizing my connection with my fellow sufferers, and I told him how energizing it had been to realize that we were survivors rather than victims.

He wanted to know more about the training itself. How had it proceeded? I told him about safe spaces and self-care. I told him about growing the movement, and about leaderful networks, and about Danutia and Emeretta.

He said, "Sounds like you didn't particularly care for them. Or am I putting words in your mouth?"

"No, Emeretta was all right, but I thought Danutia was too PC and too touchy feely. I didn't think she was properly calibrated for a room full of survivors, and other people I talked to (Vicky!) felt the same way."

That was interesting, very interesting, because he'd come to understand that his success with people—anyone's success, for that matter—originated from a place of personal power. And he knew that the only thing one could do with such a gift was share it. Otherwise, it would die. That was why, in his past couple of years in Illinois, and now here, he'd been working as a life coach and motivational speaker.

"If there was dissatisfaction with the last facilitator, maybe I could help. I'd really like to help. Do you think you could explore something like that with the people at the National Victim Alliance?"

I told him I'd talk to my bosses at National, but did he really think that would be the most effective way to approach them? I was, after all, only a volunteer. He nodded solemnly, brow furrowed, then brightened.

"I don't know why I put it that way. I've got a state-of-the-art CV. I could work up a proposal in no time. Why don't you just send me their contact information and I'll take care of the rest?"

I said I could do that. In the meantime, I told him, he should contact Mindy at Americans Together. She could certainly find a place for someone with his tech savvy. We exchanged cards and promised to follow up with emails soon. But we never did.

Because, as satisfying at the conversation had seemed when we were sitting in Dunkin' Donuts, it felt increasingly weird as I drove home. I thought back over what Dennis had said and the way it had flowed, and the more I thought about it, the more I felt I'd been diddled in some obscure way. Did he really want Danutia's job? Why bother asking me? Why the half-hour life story?

Back at the Book Palace I Googled him, and after a while I found a Dennis Sykes in Chicagoland who had a good chance of being my Dennis Sykes, age-wise and job-wise. Next, in possession of his DOB and middle initial (thanks to Ancestry.com), I surfed through Silicon Valley in search of the Stanford connection. There, amid the digital remnants of his several business endeavors (including his run as a motivational speaker) was:

UNITED STATES v. SYKES
United States District Court,
San Francisco California

The original one-count indictment in this case charged the defendant, Dennis A. Sykes, with a violation of 18 U.S.C. § 1716(h) (mailing an explosive device with intent to kill). The indictment alleged that the defendant constructed a bomb and caused it to be mailed to Lyle Simons, the defendant's supervisor at Aerotek Inc. in San Jose. The parcel was removed. It exploded upon impact and caused substantial property damage; however, no one was injured. Postal inspectors conducted an investigation of this incident, which led to the return of the original indictment by the grand jury...

Just one among the millions of bad things that happened every day, but the case had attained Internet immortality because of the issues it raised about "exculpatory no" and other legal niceties that escaped me. At that point I walked away and never looked back.

Well, I did look one last time.

I peeked over my shoulder and there he was, smiling affably in his business casual getup, behind a cup of Dunkin' Donuts decaf. I wondered what kind of splendid fuckedupness connected the bomb, the suicide, the farm, the several business startups, the speaking career, and Americans Together? Mr. Dennis A. Sykes, life coach and mad bomber, became my accomplice that afternoon, though of course he never knew it.

The call came late one April morning. I had the Boston Marathon, a surprisingly engaging spectator event, on the TV in the living room and, as the Africans (beautiful, strange creatures, constructed of nothing but legs and lungs) ran away from the rest of the field, I puttered around the house, wondering if I should, and finally deciding not to, take the Christmas candles out of the windows. The phone's ring made me jump. I walked across the hallway and looked at the number displayed on the handset. Didn't recognize it, but I answered anyway. Always the damned telephone. Always me picking it up. Maybe, if I ever succeed in going back through that membrane to the other side of time, I'll get rid of telephones.

It was Richard Winters's public defender. At the time of the trial, Bethany and I had hated this lawyer and his sniveling, obsequious manner. He was, after all, defending of our son's killer. However, I got to know him in the course of researching my book, and he turned out to be a genuinely humble person who was performing a distasteful task to the best of his ability because he believed in the system.

He apologized for coming back into our lives. I told him Bethany and I were no longer together and he apologized for that, too. He told me that he wouldn't have bothered us—me—but that something extraordinary had occurred. However, it was something that could wait. If I'd rather he call at some other time... I asked him, please, to tell me whatever he had to tell. He took a breath and told me that, after years of being in denial, Richard Winters had experienced an awakening. He wanted to contact me. He wanted to acknowledge the terrible thing he'd done. He wanted to tell me how sorry he was that he'd done it.

I held the receiver at arm's length and squinted at it, battered nearly as hard by what I'd just heard as I had been by the death call so many years before, but back in the other direction, as it were. Bruises on both sides now.

That night I called Billy and Doreen Winters. You'd know, if you read *Goodbye, My Son*, that Bethany and I had reached out to the killer's parents after the shootings. In fact, if I do say so myself, that was one of the book's more touching moments. We knew that they had suffered a blow that was, if anything, worse than the one we'd endured. Our only son was safe in heaven dead, while theirs was alive, insane, and shaming them.

Doreen answered the phone. In person she was a warm, outgoing lady. But whenever I called, I could never get more than a single sentence out of her, which invariably was, "Lemme git Billy fer ya."

"Billy. It's Joe."

"Joe! I bin thinkin you might call. How you bin?"

"I've been great, Billy. Things are terrific here."

"Ahm so glad to hear that."

"But Billy. I've got to ask you. I mean, you know why I'm calling. What happened to your son? Why does he want to talk to me now, after all this time?"

"Joe, he read yer book."

I could see life spinning slowly, a magnificent gyre, full of stuff, like the gigantic garbage patch (they always say "the size of Texas") in the middle of the Pacific Ocean. *Someone*, after all, had read my book. Someone had gotten my message, and of all the someones in the world, there could not have been a more unlikely one than Richard Winters. Perhaps, unbeknownst to myself, I'd been writing to him all along.

A couple of weeks later I received from the killer a comprehensive and tightly-structured admission of guilt, accompanied by an equally well-assembled apology. A total of two paragraphs occupying three-quarters of a page, in his morbidly precise, tightly-aligned handwriting. Richard told me that when he read about our family in my book, something in him woke up. He'd never known what a real family was, and he realized, too late, the damage he'd done. He knew Mrs. Mooney and I hated him. He knew he deserved to be hated and did not want to change that. But he had to write and apologize.

I wrote back and told him that he had given me a great deal to think about. I started the letter "Dear Richard" but then got rid of the "Dear," which seemed out of place when addressing the murderer of one's son. I told him that Ryan's death had inspired me to become active in the movement to end gun violence in America. He wrote back and told me that buying the gun—the ease with which he was able to buy that gun—was the worst thing about that night, the worst thing that ever happened to him.

Every Saturday afternoon, if I wasn't traveling, Hank and I would have what we jokingly referred to as a staff meeting. I'd get a six pack and a bag of chips and we'd sit around his desk and shoot the shit.

I told Hank what had happened.

"He's a psychopath, Joe. Zero empathy." Hank had majored in psychology, of all things, at Columbia.

"What if my book really did get through to him?"

"What if he's just bored?"

It was one of our more productive staff meetings.

I knew that people like Richard could be cunning and manipulative, and I had no way of telling if he was gaming me. I called his public defender back, and he referred me to one of the shrinks who'd examined Richard in preparation for their failed insanity defense.

I remembered the shrink, a heavy-set fellow named Rodgers who worked his hands when he talked, in a manner that suggested he was making string figures with his sentences. I called him and he told me he hadn't interviewed the Winters boy since the trial, but that people in Richard's condition sometimes responded well to a highly-structured environment that was low on stimuli—a place like prison, in other words. It seemed credible to him that, once the florid phase of the psychosis passed, Richard's mental state might have begun to improve. I should be wary, of course, but it was possible that Richard was telling the truth.

As he spoke, I imagined, not for the first time, Richard getting raped in the shower, becoming the bitch of some jailhouse Jabba the Hutt. But on this occasion, something weird happened. Not weird like Hallie and Bethany. I mean epochally weird.

Just as Richard was bending over to pick up that bar of soap, I started thinking about the whole Charles Whitman thing again. I admit to having done a little research into the fabled Texas Tower shooting when I got back from Austin, not in any obsessive way, but to better understand the strange vision that had overtaken me as I walked through the campus that night. And what I particularly remembered was, not crazy Charlie shooting people, but his father-in-law, Raymond Leissner, father of the wife Charlie loved so dearly that he stabbed her in the chest five times as she slept, in order to spare her the distress that his subsequent actions were sure to cause.

Dr. Rodgers was still talking. I thanked him and hung up.

I don't know if I can explain the transformation that came over me at that moment. In the complex and instantaneous process of my self-ministration, some little hook of a thing way down in my gut straightened out—the cumulative result of my bitter, rage-filled years of investigation into the causes of my son's death, triggered by this gesture from his murderer, but also by the maturity of my own formulation of something Charlie's father-in-law said years after Whitman had killed his daughter:

It's done. It's over with. It's gone. There's no use trying to find out why... I got my consolement from Almighty God. I kind of left it in his hands. That's the only way to live a decent life.

A decent life!

In the weeks and months that followed this strange recognition, Almighty God and I discussed what a decent life might entail, as well as this business with Ryan's murderer, at great length and to considerable effect. When He spoke, it was like a breeze blowing through a curtain.

You are but a grain of sand on an endless beach, He told me.

And He said, *Every happening has its cause, and each cause is fed by streams of prior causes fed by rivers springing from oceans of causes. You will drown in causes. Understanding is Vanity. Forgiveness is Vanity.*

And He said, *Everyone has a story.*

JANUARY ?
—SENATOR SAWTELLE

If it hadn't been for the Bouncy Castle Massacre I'm not sure I would ever have grasped the part Senator Morton Sawtelle played in the promulgation of gun violence.

As you may recall, that horrific event grabbed its week's worth of headlines not because of the number killed (six children) but for the grotesque way the killings took place. Somehow the guy got a pistol into the play area next to a Chuckie Cheese. Killed three kids outside, then went into the Bouncy Castle and shot a seven-year-old, whereupon the air went out and the castle collapsed on them, suffocating him and two other children in a most hideous manner. You may remember all this, but why would you want to? Anyway, there was a gigantic forest fire in California the next week, and the crazed killer sank into the obscurity he deserved, except in the minds and lives of the dead children's parents and relatives, and teachers and playmates, who did not deserve any of it.

Thanks to those grisly headlines it dawned on Congress that there might be more to the gun violence issue than arguing about the defining characteristics of the assault rifle. However, their attention was diverted, or maybe enhanced, by the suicide of a Congressman's daughter. Early reports said she'd used the Congressman's improperly secured pistol to do the deed, but those rumors were soon squelched. The House of Representatives declared a moment of silence in honor of the daughter, after which the Democrats went back to their constituents for a round of widely-heralded "Fact Finding" sessions about gun violence. The Republicans, with some justification, called it a publicity stunt.

In our state Senator Perkins (the son of my old friend and mentor), Representative Crowley, and Representative Hart scheduled a Round Table event at which they planned to meet with survivors of gun violence to hear their personal stories and their suggestions about how to address the problem. Televised and live-streamed on social media, of course, so everyone was able to bear witness to what ensued.

Perkins's office called The Church of Zion, looking for help in rounding up suitable survivors, and Barbara Jackson nominated me.

"I've got four ladies from the Enduring Memory Sisters," she said, "Inner city folks. And Americans Together sent me two survivor moms from the suburbs.

But I'm having a hard time finding any men. Do you want to talk to the politicians?"

"Will there be food?"

"Oh, shush."

We gathered in a meeting room on the top floor of the Harborside Hotel. The sun sparkling off the water shot the room through with shards of light. Before we all sat down, I had the pleasure of telling Senator Perkins that I'd known his father. He treated me to a warm smile and a firm handshake and said, "Yes, I know," which made me feel terrific. You watch professional athletes on TV and they look pretty much like anyone else. Then, when you see them in real life, they look like demigods or creatures from another race. Politicians are like that. They have something we normals do not.

We milled around the table (it was actually round), whites on one side, blacks on the other. It wasn't oppositional in any way, just that talking about dead children was difficult, and the Enduring Memory Sisters were staying close, supporting one another. Eventually we found our seats, whereupon each of the politicians made an angry speech about how gun violence was tearing our country apart and how the Republicans, led by NRA sock puppet Senator Morton Sawtelle, were letting it happen. I recalled the name, but until that moment I hadn't understood the degree to which he'd been instrumental in pushing those gun laws through Congress. Judging by the gusto with which each of them ripped into him, Senator Sawtelle was bad guy numero uno.

After that we went around the table sharing our stories. Another miserable misuse of words, now that I think of it. If somebody shoves a plate of shit in front of you, are they "sharing" it?

Unfortunately, my story about Ryan's death was rather incoherent. The politicians must've assumed that my many sufferings had turned my brain to yogurt. In fact, I'd become profoundly distracted by the news that Universal Concealed Carry had been Sawtelle's baby. This occasioned my second-favorite fantasy loop, the one in which I line Sawtelle, Henry Becker, and Arthur Freedman up against a wall and...

The two suburban moms told heart-rending stories of teenage suicide, but those ladies from the ghetto just blew everyone away. They wanted to be damned sure the politicians felt their pain and their rage, which were so intense as to be undifferentiated. Like when you smash your thumb with a hammer, and you're holding the throbbing joint, and you're screaming. Is the pain foremost, or the rage?

The first lady's son was Biggie McCall. She held a photograph of him, as if she were cradling her baby. They called him Biggie because he weighed 300. Solid. He was eighteen. There were gangs in each housing complex, but he didn't belong. Didn't need to. One of his friends got into a tussle with a kid from the gang in the next complex and beat him up. The friend came to Biggie, terrified that the gang would come after him. Biggie gave him cab fare and told him to get out of there. The gang followed Biggie's sister home, right up the sidewalk. As he went out to get her, they started shooting. They shot up the whole front of the house. Biggie ran but they got him between two cars. One shot, in the back, severed an aorta. She worked in the hospital. They called her. She drove home and there he was in the street in a pool of blood. She ran to him. She wanted to touch her baby, kiss him, help him. But the cop on the scene said Biggie had already passed, and he would not let her touch him. The body lay there on the pavement for ten hours before more Poh-leese came with an ambulance and took him away.

Senator Perkins and Representative Hart made notes on their yellow legal pads, grim faced. The third Representative, Crowley, was an elderly fellow in a dark blue suit. He looked like a mortician. Perfect. They were perfect, those pols, and the white suicide mothers, and the ghetto ladies from Enduring Memory. Everyone looked exactly like who they were.

Except for Claire, the tall, slender, dark one in the tight white dress. She had a striking, manly face, and could have been a female impersonator, but she was not. Her son had been shot by a kid who'd bullied him at school. The bully's gang was taunting her son, and the bully had a gun and started shooting it off, just to scare him, but one hit him in the head. They said it was an accident. He lay in a coma for two days and the people at the hospital worked desperately to save him, but there was nothing they could do. They told her, Claire, his brain is dead. Then she had to decide whether to pull the plug. And she decided that her boy had been so lively and active that he shouldn't have to lay there for how long like a vegetable waiting for a miracle to happen in a world where there were no miracles. So she told them to pull the plug, and now she has to live with that decision. Every day. "He dies every day," she told us. "I die every day." Each of the ladies showed a color photograph of her murdered son. Claire's fourteen-year-old was the handsomest of them all. She donated his organs and he saved the lives of three people.

Nadine Hampton was the leader of the Enduring Memory Sisters. Her son had been killed sixteen years earlier, victim of a bullet intended for someone else. They never found the killer. They never looked. She could never get any Poh-leese interested in the case. So she decided she'd take matters into her own hands. "I would have killed the coward myself," she said, and we believed she could have. "Except I didn't want no more killing. There was killing all around us. Too much killing." She started going out on the streets. That was how the sisterhood of Enduring Memory had begun. Other women like Claire who'd had children murdered were with her right out there in the bad neighborhoods. They weren't afraid. The worst thing that could have happened to them had already happened. They went into schools, too.

Nadine said, "We're tired of black people killing black people and the murders not being solved. We are block takers. We are taking over, one block at a time. And we'll be packing, too—school supplies, help with groceries, hugs, and love." When the sisters heard about another mother, they reached out to her and took her in.

Sitting between the mortician and Nadine was a lady who obviously was not one of the Enduring Memory Sisters—the hugs were different and there was no small talk. She was plain-featured, very dark skinned. Black hair semi-straight. No jewelry or ornamentation.

From her bag she pulled a piece of cardboard, about the size of the 8 x 10 photos the other mothers had. But this one unfolded like a triptych. She opened it and showed it around the table, then put it in front of her and began to speak.

"This is my daughter Shannon. She was just fifteen. She was walking home with her boyfriend. A dealer who had a beef with him shot them with a Tec-9. She was hit three times. I bring this picture with me whenever I talk to legislators about guns, because this is what they're legislating about. Not laws or rights. *This*."

A crime scene photo, obviously. God knows how she'd gotten it. The daughter had her legs curled under her but her back was flat on the pavement and her arms thrown out. White top and blue jeans. A small puddle of dark red blood beside her. Her face was twisted in the other direction from the way her torso was turned, as if it had been trying to escape her body. She had the same dark complexion and semi-straight hair as her mom. She might have been pretty but you couldn't tell for sure because her left eye had been destroyed. Entrance wounds aren't usually very dramatic, but the exploded eye was terrible to behold. Her fists were clenched, which somehow made it seem worse.

You could have heard a pin drop.

My correspondence with Ryan's killer stumbled along. There were, of course, terrifying minefields of complication, implication, to be avoided at all costs. What could he say? That I was obliged to hate him? To kill him? What could I tell him? That everyone has a story? *It's done. "I"s over with. It's gone. There's no use trying to find out why...* I just had to be careful, very careful, not to let these newly discovered truths overwhelm me, trick me. I had to keep reminding myself that I had not, by some impenetrably mysterious process, swapped my son's killer for my son. Richard was still who he was, and he was running his game, and I was who I was, running mine, and we were no more than grains of sand.

In due course Richard Winters and I agreed to use our joint story to try to ensure that others would not have to suffer through similar stories. I would pursue my work with Americans Together, and my news appearances, speeches, and essays, and Richard would tell whoever would listen—mostly shrinks and documentary film makers, although *Newsweek* quoted him once—He told them that the ease with which he'd been able to buy that gun, even when he was in the midst of a mental breakdown, was the worst thing that ever happened to him. We traded bits of information, sporadically at first, about the progress of our joint campaign.

Then I received a letter from Richard that said, in part, "There is a new book out called *Ritual Violence*. It's a psychological explanation of school shootings and there's a whole chapter about my crime. I had someone send me the book and I discovered that it plagiarizes from *Goodbye, My Son...* I'm just personally offended that he didn't even attempt to interview me for the book, but that's my narcissism speaking."

Well, that piqued *my* narcissism. I bought a copy of the book and read it. And sure enough, the writer had stolen my stuff. When I confronted the lazy bastard, he confessed to his crimes and slunk back into his hole. I published an exposé of his work. You can still read it on Amazon, among other places. A few weeks later I received a distraught letter from Richard Winters. He told me he felt terrible. Not only had he damaged so many lives with his shooting, now he was responsible for ruining the reputation of the sociologist. I told him not to worry, that the plagiarist had done sloppy work, and that he'd been right to call attention to this. Richard wrote back, greatly relieved, and I returned to

my meditations on the mysteries of a decent life—this
time to ponder the bizarre situation in which I comfort
the murderer of my son.

Examples of everything happening for a reason abound. My reunion with Barbara Jackson happened shortly after I began communicating with my son's killer. It's more than irony.

For the first year following Ryan's murder I gave passionate, tearful speeches against gun violence at marches, vigils, and rallies. There were enough of them to choose from, God knows. Each event featured appearances by supportive politicians and fire-breathing organizers, followed by survivors courageously sharing their stories. If reporters were on the scene, we survivors sought their cameras, certain that our pain would inspire people to get off their duffs and do something about gun violence. But the rallies, as important and exhilarating as they seemed to us, never escaped the thin crowd of friends, relatives, and true believers gathered around the platform, collars turned up against the chilly breeze.

Barbara Jackson stood out from the run of victim story-sharers at these events. She was, as I've mentioned, a powerful speaker. We were both fresh in our grief in those early days, and we bonded. However, once I started doing the research for *Goodbye, My Son,* there didn't seem to be enough time for those rallies. Barbara and I lost touch until, perhaps inevitably, we met again at a conference on urban gun violence to which I had been sent by Americans Together.

She was standing in the midst of a group of people of color, next to a table manned by staffers of an organization called The Healing Collaborative. A little rounder, a little grayer, but still unmistakably Barbara. As politely as I could, I edged through the crowd and found a place beside the minister to whom she was speaking. Everyone turned to look at me. I felt very white. Barbara studied me intently, then cocked her head back and broke into that smile.

"Now, there's a face I know!"

"Joe Mooney, Barbara. It's wonderful to see you again."

She put her generous shoulders against mine and squeezed. I squeezed back. "People, this man here and I have something in common, and I think you know what it is."

Nodding heads and a murmur from the group.

"And this was from years ago, people. This man had the courage to see past his own troubles."

She asked how I'd been and I told her things were

great. I told her I'd gotten involved with Americans Together, and I told her about the work I was doing for them, establishing a National Victim Alliance Network in support of sensible gun laws. I told her I'd written a best-selling book about Ryan's murder. I told her I was continuing my investigations into the problem of gun violence in America, and that I'd written several articles about it. I told her I was in correspondence with my son's killer and that we were working together to get the message out about the consequences of weak gun laws.

Barbara looked around her circle of her friends as if to say, *See what I mean?* She reached down, grabbed a flier from the table and thrust it into my hand. "You've got to come see what we've done!"

Then the lights flashed, signaling the start of the second session, and we returned to the auditorium. I was delighted to have bumped into my old comrade, and I really did mean to visit her, but once again my gun studies distracted me. It wasn't until the live-feed suicides began appearing on Facebook that I showed up at her door, bereft, begging for I didn't know what.

Those ghastly videos had pitched me into some kind of crisis. How could they not have? I know we suffered as a nation, but the hideous spectacle of teenagers shooting themselves in public had a particularly dispiriting effect on me. My teen's life had been stolen from him, and here these kids were, throwing theirs away. In public, no less. It was too hideous to contemplate. Auto-snuff segments were going up as fast as they could be taken down, and all Americans Together could do was advocate for background checks. The disconnect was profound. Tiny fissures appeared in the movement. Factions began to develop. Battles broke out on Facebook and Twitter. I became disoriented. Miserable weeks passed before I remembered the flier Barbara had given me.

The Church of Zion was a squat, gray stone structure with a wooden el strung out behind it, the recycled sanctuary of a wealthier congregation from a better day. A wide stone stairway led from the sidewalk up to elaborately carved double doors beneath a heaven of dusty stained glass, from which a security camera peered like the eye of God. The windows at street level were covered with plywood.

Barbara met me at the door and gave me a tour of the chapel, the therapy rooms, the day care center, the cafeteria and meeting spaces, and the two offices, crowded with people talking on phones or hunched over computers. The Healing Collaborative, of which she was the founder and CEO, was the community outreach branch of the Church of Zion. They had relationships with major inner-city hospitals, and they provided in-house counseling and referrals to over one thousand victims a year. When there was a fatal shooting, a call would go out and the Collaborative would send trained responders to support that family, night and day if need be. They had a youth program that visited local high schools teaching the basics of conflict resolution and social justice. They were endorsed by the District Attorney, the Chief of Police, and the Attorney General. They worked with the criminal justice system to educate victims about their rights, and about how criminal cases proceeded. They assisted families in managing their grief and pain, and provided help with more mundane things, like what to do when you have to bury your fourteen-year-old son.

A thousand victims a year!

Her office was a clutter of boxes, books, and file folders. The image of Barbara's son Cooper smiled down on us from a framed color photo on the wall. The same image adorned the covers of the pamphlets heaped on her desk. The boy was dead, but he was not lost.

Barbara told me they had a healthy list of donors, and were receiving grant money, but the need was great, and the work never stopped. She plucked a pamphlet from the pile. "This is one we just finished. We call it *Working Within the Criminal Justice System*, but really it's about knowing your rights. Some people never get their child's belongings back. Can you imagine? Clothing, jewelry. Impounded and destroyed after the trial with no thought of its meaning to the family. People need help with that."

"How can I help you?" I asked, "How can Americans Together help you?" I lusted after her thousand victims for my chapter of the National Victim Alliance.

I told her that there were many community and faith-based operations doing wonderful work—the Healing Collaborative was doing wonderful work—but only Americans Together worked throughout all fifty states. I told her we could give her Healing Collaborative prominence in the gun wars, a national platform from which their people would be able to share their stories. Americans Together had public relations experts and strategists. We could help publicize the work the Collaborative was doing, help advocate for funding.

Barbara said, "I think that's wonderful, what your people are doing. But that's not what we're doing. That's not what we're about."

"Not about stopping gun violence?" My ignorance did not require elaboration, but I jabbered on. "America needs to know about your people. The invisible ones. The ones who lose their children on the streets. We can give them a voice."

"We're not political, Joe. Groups like Americans Together, Brady, Gifford's, Stop Handgun Violence—if they want our help, we'll give it, sure. But I'm honoring my son in a different way. When Cooper died, I saw that the community had a need, and we got busy trying to fill it. Now you want to come in here and offer us... what? People of privilege, Joe. People from the outside, they have no idea what goes on here. They already have the resources they need. They're off with their psychiatrists and life coaches and support groups. They're at the gym, on a golf course. They're healing. My people, the people in this city, they don't have the resources to do that. All they've got is us. Your people want to come and learn, you want to come and lend a hand, sure. We need all the help we can get. But no national alliance of folks from the suburbs is going to do anything for us here."

People of privilege. Was that where I lived?

"There's the moment of violence, Joe. That's where all the noise comes from. That's where the battle over gun control is being fought—that single moment of the violent act. But that's not where we work. Because there's all the time *before* that moment of violence, and all the time *after* it. How did it get to murder? Who takes care of survivors? That's what we're interested in. All the time before, and all the time after."

I staggered out of the Church of Zion carrying the weight of... of more than just her words. The task was clear to me, and it was a mighty one.

All this time (all the time before) I'd been convinced that political action was the means by which we'd put an end to gun violence. We simply needed to force Congress to pass laws restricting people's ability to get their hands on guns, and then a few more laws that would make people legally responsible for the guns they already owned, and lives would be saved.

Well, more than just a few laws. Laws in every state of the Union. Rammed down the throats of fanatics who in a sick way are half right. Gun death requires people for its completion. That was the difficult part. That was where Americans Together got stuck.

Now I could see gun violence as a disease that infested vulnerable communities. Barbara Jackson and her people were in there like penicillin, like antibodies on sick cells. How did it get to murder? How do we help survivors be other than vengeful, dysfunctional perpetrators of a broken society? How do we interrupt the cycle of violence?

I mailed her a check for $2500.

After the *Ritual Violence* plagiarism incident, it became clear to me that Richard Winters and I really were, in some fundamental way, working together to get the message out about gun violence. And if that were the case, shouldn't the father of a murdered son and the son's killer—locked up for life—be making better use of their dramatic assets? Americans Together was all about story sharing. Didn't Richard and I have a hell of a story? Maybe Mindy or Cliff could get *Newsweek* to come back for a longer interview with the killer and me. Or the *New York Times*. Hell, they'd published a letter of mine already.

The idea of a prison visit had occurred to me while I was working on my book, but at that time Richard had presented himself as an unrepentant lunatic. In fact, as I learned from our lawyer, he was furious because his public defender would not look more thoroughly into Ryan's background. Richard was convinced that some evil thing in Ryan's past had caused God to select him to be murdered. What could I say to that?

Now the situation was different. Richard and I had things to discuss. Our meeting itself would send a powerful message, one on which we might both elaborate. I found the appropriate person at the Department of Correction, a woman named Connors, who was the chief of Victim Services. We met in her office at state headquarters, and within five minutes she'd thrown me out on my ear.

She began by reiterating what she had already told me in the course of several telephone conversations: that there was currently no program for victims to meet with the inmates who had victimized them, or for victims to tour facilities in which their offenders were housed. Could I imagine the chaos that might ensue if an offender and a victim were accidentally to meet in this setting?

I told her I could not imagine any such chaos and I asked her if she were implying that DOC could not control their inmates. She replied that the motivating factor in DOC's policy was "security," and that they were protecting victims by keeping them away from institutions in which their offenders were housed.

I lapsed into dumbfoundedness.

Sensing that, for whatever reason, I was too dim to grasp this simplest of explanations, she told me there was something else I could do, another course of action I might take to help me satisfy my needs in this difficult situation. I asked what she had in mind. She told me that I could drive past the prison and look at it.

I asked her if she were informing me that I, a citizen of the United States, might get in my car and drive it on a public road? If so, she was telling me something I already knew. But Ms. Connors had not finished sharing information about Victim Services.

"I want to be honest with you," she told me.

"Please do," I replied.

"I want to be honest," she repeated, "When anybody, like you, expresses interest in a particular inmate or a particular institution, I am required to report it to that institution. I don't have to tell you this, but I want you to know." There was another pause, signaling her effort to find the appropriate words. "Don't try to get in there and see him. You'll get in serious trouble."

I asked her if she could she imagine what it meant to live a decent life?

She declared the conversation at an end.

I told her I wanted to speak to her superior.

She told me again that our meeting was over, and that if I didn't leave on my own, she would have me escorted out. As I was heading for the door, I asked her what she was so afraid of? She did not reply. I then asked if she didn't have better things to do than hatch dimwitted paranoid fantasies.

I suppose I did get a little carried away, but that

woman's attitude seemed so wrong. What was the Department of Correction supposed to be correcting if there was no room in their program for reconciliation? Prison, I knew, was like grad school for criminals. Recidivism was at shameful levels, and this woman was abetting it all.

Mister Farrell

That very afternoon news of the South Carolina Chicken Plant Shooting came out. As you might imagine, this did not improve my turbulent emotional state. I took a bike ride, trying to calm my writhing brain. A couple of kids on the sidewalk saw me and shouted, "Hi, mister Farrell!" I smiled and waved back.

The mister Farrell thing had started in my jogging days and carried over to my cycling career. Jim Farrell was a shop teacher at the high school, and a genuine good egg. He also happened to look a great deal like me. Which led to our being mistaken for one another when jogging or cycling around the neighborhood. He didn't look like me to me, nor I like him to him, but Bethany said he did, and his wife agreed. We'd bump into them at Little League games—they had a son a year younger than Ryan—and we'd joke about it. He'd call me Jim and I'd call him Joe. Silly stuff like that. We had them over a couple of times, and they had us over. The boys got along pretty well, and we hit it off as couples. Nothing too intense, but fun. Jim liked to have a drink. After Ryan died, they were at our door with dinners, to sit with us in quiet misery like that UU minister Walter.

The perpetrator of the Chicken Plant Shooting had used a paperclip to make his AR fire on full auto, but he'd been intent on vengeance rather than mass murder. He was after the line boss and the shift manager, with whom he'd had prior issues that had resulted in his being fired. He found the manager first and shot him at close range with the AR, expending most of a thirty-round magazine in an eyeblink and distributing the poor manager's body parts among the chicken parts. Eye witnesses said it was a horrendous scene. He also wounded two nearby line workers. It is difficult for someone without training to control the fire of a fully automatic rifle, so there were unintended casualties. Then, of course, the jury-rigged paper clip device failed. He went after the line boss with a revolver and put three slugs in him before blowing his own brains out. Because there were only two fatalities—three, depending on how you counted—it didn't really qualify as a mass shooting. But, as you probably recall, it got plenty of news coverage because the shooter was an illegal alien. Heads rolled at the Chicken Plant when that information came out, but it was too late for the line boss, and it was too late for the dismembered manager, who'd hired him illegally in the first place.

The same question was on everyone's mind: *How did*

he get the guns if he was an illegal alien? But it was a rhetorical question because everyone knew he got the guns from some guy in a parking lot, or maybe from a bad apple at a gun show. Gun control people were outraged. Another loophole!

Republicans and the NRA accused them of taking advantage of a tragic killing for propaganda purposes. Both were right, but the gun control people were righter.

When I finished my bike ride, I went on YouTube to look through the dozens of videos that demonstrated the ways one could convert a semi-automatic AR into one capable of firing on full auto, but I couldn't concentrate on them. I kept thinking back to that nasty lady at the DOC, and her idiotic warning about sneaking into prison. Then I thought about the kids mistaking me for Jim Farrell, and then I saw what I would do. A missile. Just like when I was writing the book.

Saturday afternoon I brought a six pack over to Jim's house and told him my idea. He already knew about my correspondence with Richard; the whole town knew about it. I think the Angels approved of my reaching out to Ryan's killer, although Bethany was mystified and, in that quiet way of hers, pissed off. She told me I was making a travesty of our son's death. We didn't talk about it after that.

Jim was more sympathetic. "So, you take my driver's license and pose as me, and walk into prison and visit the kid who killed Ryan?"

"Yup. If they catch me, I'll say I stole it from you."

"Why?"

"Because I can."

"You mean because you can't."

"Exactly."

"You're working on another book, aren't you?"

Good old Jim! Until that moment I hadn't thought about writing a sequel. My humiliation at the failure of *Goodbye, My Son* had been too complete. Suddenly, just like that night of the death call, I could see the whole thing. America loved a second act. This would be a redemption story. Richard and Joe. Two tortured souls finding their way to peace through forgiveness. Humane, courageous, and with a plot twist revealing the ineptitude of the Department of Correction. I gave Jim a sly nod.

"The killer and I are working together to get the message out about guns."

Then something unexpected happened. My mouth kept moving. "In fact, we're going to make an anti-gun commercial together. I'll get him on camera right in his cell, and he'll say, *When I was so crazy I thought God was commanding me to kill people, it was still a simple matter for me to walk into a gun store and buy an assault rifle.* He's told me that a dozen times. We'll put it on YouTube. It'll go viral."

"Jesus, Joe. That's powerful!"

He was right. It was a brilliant idea. A gut punch to America's flabby midsection. One minute I'm lying to Jim in order to secure his complicity, and the next minute I win by a knockout.

On I go, spooling my twisty yarn, and you're reading patiently along, wondering when I'm going to get around to explaining those bizarre murders. What can I tell you? These people and moments are teeth in a ratchet that only ratchets one way, which is tighter. The lid was off. The barn door was open and the toothpaste was not going back in. All the while I sought to consume the problem of gun violence, it was consuming me. My *Boston Globe* is not on the porch. I think someone has stolen it.

The more I thought about my prison visitation scheme the better it got. Our back story—Joe Mooney and Richard Winters seeking redemption through forgiveness—was powerful. The point of it—Richard's confession about how easy it had been for a crazy person to get a gun—was compelling. The subtext of the whole adventure would be the father of the murdered son sneaking into prison and sitting down with the murderer—that just might be a sharp enough dart to penetrate America's complacent hide.

There was just one problem.

Becoming Jim Farrell seemed simple enough, but the prospect of sitting down with Ryan's killer, now that I had figured out a way to do it, made me woozy. It was like quicksand. Each time I approached it I got woozier. I couldn't find any firm ground. The instant I imagined myself facing him I'd start to sink. Then Bethany came along and saved me. Not that she intended to. It just worked out that way.

I walked into the Book Palace one day and there she was, shooting the shit with Hank. She'd bring him a cup of coffee every once in a while; as I said, they were quite fond of one another. That was fine, I understood. But for some reason it always upset me to see her talking with him. So it was my habit to make myself scarce during her visits.

This time, as I was heading for the back room she said, "We need to talk."

"Okay..."

Hank skedaddled.

"We're selling the house, Joe. I'm selling the house."

What was I supposed to say to that?

"I talked to Mom about it. She knows about us now. You and I will split the proceeds." Curt Parkingham probably would have been against giving me a nickel, but he had Alzheimer's and was slipping fast. Bethany's mom had always been a pushover. "And we'll get a divorce. I want to keep it as simple as possible."

"Divorce?" What else was I supposed to say?

"There's someone in my life, Joe."

"Someone in your life?"

"His name is Rex. Rex Nichols. He's a therapist on the Cape. We met online."

I said, "What am I supposed to say?" Then I said, "What about your girlfriend? What about Hallie? You just going to dump her?"

"It was never what you thought, Joe. Never anything like that."

"Bullshit."

She rolled her eyes, feigning exasperation. "It was mortifying for Hallie, just trying to do the best for both of us. You were so cruel to her."

"But you weren't cruel, eh?"

"No one could get through to you, Joe. After a while we just stopped trying. That weird gun stuff, your fantasies, it was all something you needed to do to yourself. God knows why." Ice cold.

She slit me from anus to gills and my insides plopped out. So, when it came time to visit Jeff, I'd be calm, perfectly empty.

But my prison visit got shoved to the back burner by Bethany's fanatical insistence on keeping things simple. "Simple," I came to understand, meant "fast." Which I resented. Aside from my own stuff, I didn't take much from the house—a couple of things of Ryan's, one of his skateboards, the absurd silk smoking jacket he used to enjoy wearing, a few photographs, and similar tokens of his existence. I put most of my belongings in storage and took up full-time residence in the Book Palace—at least until I could find a suitable apartment. I slept on the cot in back, used the microwave and hotplate, and Ryan's little fridge from college. Showers at the Y after a workout. It worked out fine. However, I was terribly annoyed at having been forced by the impending divorce to retain legal counsel. The thought of sharing the particulars of our relationship with a divorce lawyer disgusted me.

Then Bethany brought in one of those yard sale managers to dispose of the remaining contents of the house. We had an argument about that, our first since the terrible one. Even though I needed to be extracted from that temple of grief, I resented the manner in which she was going about it. As if nothing in our past life meant anything to her. As if it were all just stuff to be disposed of. That's how focused she was on whatever future she imagined with her shrink/boyfriend (we should all be so lucky!). And going back to grad school to become a speech therapist? You can bet Romeo put that one into her empty noggin. I told her she might as well just torch the place and move on, after which I'm afraid our argument got a little heated. There may have been some shoving involved, I don't really remember. I was too wrought up. I drove to Maine to do some book scouting, and when I got back our house was nearly empty. The rooms echoed. It gave me the creeps.

A young family soon snapped the place up. The guy was a contractor and he immediately started doing renovations over there. Pretty wife, two kids, shaggy dog, SUV, big stainless-steel barbecue in the side yard. After a few attempts to be neighborly they saw I wasn't up to it and left me alone. They must have thought I was some kind of eccentric.

Hank was miffed that I'd moved into his kingdom. No more naps in the back room for him. And I suspect Bethany told him some things that turned him against me, probably having to do with our argument over the house. She and I were both a little crazed. I'm sure I said things to her, did things that were out of line. But it was mean of her to use them against me like that. Hank was my trusted employee. I couldn't stand the way he started looking at me. Was it pity? Accusation? *What*? When I'd ask him what the matter was, he'd tell me nothing was the matter.

Things between us fell apart, thanks to my suddenly vindictive soon-to-be ex-wife. I finally told him there wasn't enough work for him and that I had to let him go for financial reasons. But he wasn't fooled. It was a sad day for both of us. When the money for the house came through, I gave him a severance package of $10,000. He gave me that look again—*What?* But he cashed the check.

The severance with Hallie was more dramatic. Everything with her was like that. I saw her outside the post office one day and tried to pretend I hadn't. She just stood there, more or less in my way. What was I supposed to say?

"I can't believe you, Joe. I don't understand you."

I felt like a bug with a pin stuck through it. "I don't know what you're talking about."

"Bethany should have a restraining order out on you right now. What in God's name do you think you're doing?"

"Right. We've got to be there for Bethany. What ever happened to that?"

"Do you have any idea how hard we worked not to lose you?"

"Stop fucking with me, Hallie."

"You're an idiot, Joe. All you ever did was embarrass yourself."

"All you ever did was fuck me over. Pretending you wanted the best for everyone. What a crock. So Bethany finally got sick of you..."

"She had to get out of that house, Joe. She could see you coming apart and it frightened her."

"Oh, spare me. Brenda and Rachel, they're not a couple?"

"That has nothing to do with it. We tried, Joe. We all tried."

"Go to hell."

I saw Rex once, from across the street, just before the house went on the market, helping Bethany take the last of her stuff away. The day of those two mosquitoes, now that I think of it. He was as unlike a manly Rex Nichols as you could imagine. Vegan skinny, owl glasses, with a pointy gray beard. Wearing sandals and socks, and he and Bethany were moving to Cape Cod. The fucking Cape!

I hadn't heard from Vicky in weeks, which meant she was going through one of her spells, which always made me nervous.

After an appropriate interval I left her a message. Then I called a couple of times, with no response. Another week went by and I began to get worried. Finally, it got so bad that I told Vicky's answering machine I was coming down there, and drove to Pettucket, expecting the worst. I got it, but not the way I'd expected.

She answered the door with a blank look, and it was clear she was still in the midst of a disturbance. The left side of her face was red and swollen and she had a bruise under her eye, a raspberry mouse that would soon blossom into an ugly purple thing.

"Jesus, Vicky. What happened?"

"I walked into a door." Scary crazy-person monotone.

I should have known as soon as I heard that classic cover-up for battery. Nobody ever got a black eye from "walking into a door." How could you even walk into a door? But like a chump, I walked into it, and it turned out to be a buzz saw. "Who did this to you? Did someone hurt you?"

She let me in and I reached out to hug her. She stepped back. "You hurt me."

"What?"

"You know perfectly well what I'm talking about, you bastard."

"Vicky..."

"I saw the pictures, Joe. You and that black bitch. You practically had your tongue in her ear."

"Pictures?"

"On Facebook. It's all over the Internet. You're fucking that Emeretta woman, aren't you?"

Any time there was a group action, Americans Together put images of the event on the Internet. I remembered lining up with Patti, Robert, and Emeretta for a series of photos in Austin, outside the State House cafeteria where the lobbyist had taken us for lunch. I supposed there must have been a few shots of Emeretta and me together. Maybe we had our arms around one another, I couldn't recall. Then there were those tagged Facebook posts after we'd bird dogged Senator Blumenthal in New Hampshire. And last June's National Gun Violence Awareness Day march in New York. I did have my arm around her that time, helping her through the crowd. My poor, dear Vicky must've searched the Internet for weeks to come up with fuel for her paranoid fantasy.

"Sweetie, this is nuts! She's half my age." It's funny, the way thoughts come up when you're under stress. Maybe it's just a matter of which particular notion strikes you out of the shitstorm of thoughts that explode in your face at such moments. I remember thinking that Emeretta was probably more like a third my age, that the other woman on the Austin trip, Patti, was more my type, and that an Austin interlude might've been fun, hotel rooms and all. "And..." (grasping for straws) And... she's *blind.*"

"Bastard. You're all out there making fun of me, aren't you? I care for you the best I can. I let you in my house. I let you in my bed. And this is the thanks I get. They all know, don't they!" I backed away, maintaining eye contact. No sudden movements. I made it to the porch and she rushed forward and slammed the door in my face. I heard the deadbolt clunk.

That was the worst it had ever been. I consoled myself, at first, thinking how sweet our reunion would be. Gradually, however, I came to realize there would be no reunion. Days went by without a word from her. I left dopey messages, trying to sound casual and concerned, but I sounded lame even to myself.

Then I got a call from Mindy at Americans Together. She and John (one of the lawyers from the Advocacy

Group) were going to be passing through Boston and they wanted to meet with me. I assumed they were going to give me a pep talk regarding my less-than-exemplary performance as Victim Alliance Coordinator. I should have known, but how could I have known?

The two of them were waiting for me in the Irish bar on the ground floor of the Lenox Hotel. The place was dark and empty, and when I saw their funereal looks, I knew I was in for it, whatever it was going to be.

We made small talk while I waited for my Guinness. I noticed they had coffees and realized that, by ordering a beer at 11 am, I had committed a minor social misstep. They studied their cups assiduously.

"So what's going on, anyway?"

Mindy looked up at me, sad eyes framed by her Dutch Boy haircut. "This is really difficult, Joe."

"Difficult? How?"

"Vicky Gimble."

"Oh, Christ. I've been worried about her. Is she all right?"

"She's complained to us about you, Joe. She says you've been stalking her, and that you, umm, forced yourself on her. She sent pictures. Selfies. She looked pretty beat up."

"She told me she walked into a door. Maybe she did,

as ridiculous as that sounds. I certainly didn't do it to her."

"But you did have some contact with her?" John was trying to sound sympathetic.

"Vicky and I have been going out for a year or so. We met at the training right here in Boston."

"Why do you think she'd make these allegations?"

"It's part of her cycle. She gets paranoid and she needs someone to lash out against. I always flattered myself that I could take it. Kind of proud of it, to tell you the truth. Like I was helping. I'm very fond of her. I know she's got issues, but I never thought..."

"Yes, we're aware of the issues. Honestly, Joe, we're not sure that her story, as she presents it, is one hundred percent accurate."

"About my beating her up? One hundred percent inaccurate."

"I mean her story about her parents. She was a ward of the state at some point, and there were domestic violence issues subsequent to that, possibly a suicide, though we don't know where the 'Gimble' surname came from. We'll need to do more digging, but it's clear the story she presents in her bio is fabricated to some degree. There's no real vetting process for people in the National Victim Alliance. (Dennis!) It just never occurred to us that anyone would misrepresent themselves in such a manner. I suppose we're lucky that something like this hasn't happened before."

"Well, if she's got mental issues and she's inventing her story, what does that say about her complaint against me?" It was odd that I'd never considered the possibility that Vicky was actually, literally, crazy. Damaged, sure. But that was part of her tragic allure.

"We understand, Joe." I thought Mindy was going to put her hand on mine, but she must've had second thoughts about human contact. It plopped in the middle of the table like a delicate dead fish. "But we can't afford to have this blow up in our faces. We're a fledgling organization, and we've been working hard to establish our credibility. If she files charges, brings in the law, tries to take us to court—no matter how groundless her allegations prove to be—we'll suffer great harm. The movement will suffer."

The beer tasted skunky. I knew I should have been infuriated by this political bullshit, but I felt the same thing I felt when I found out about Bethany and Hallie. Which is to say, nothing but sick emptiness. Never order the first Guinness of the day.

"We know how much you've done for us, Joe. You'll never lose our friendship, support, respect, but…"

"But."

They terminated me as State Victim Alliance Coordinator, lawyered up, and let Vicky know that, in the course of investigating her charges against me, they'd uncovered serious, possibly fraudulent, discrepancies in her story about the murder-suicide of her parents. Then we held our collective breaths and waited for Vicky Gimble to disappear.

The nothingness soon gave way to a devastation so severe that I longed, in vain, for nothing to return. The staff at Americans Together showered me with condolences. We all make sacrifices, Mindy told me, and I'd been forced by circumstances to make the biggest one. I'd taken a hit for the team, and they felt terrible about it.

I felt worse.

Vicky was batshit crazy, a danger to herself and others. She had lied to me, used me, and taken advantage of me in some way and for some reason I could not comprehend. Still, I missed her terribly. I missed the sex, sure. But I missed her mind even more. I didn't care how screwed up she was, or even that her story was partly fabricated. She *saw* things. Valuable things. True things. *There's nothing left of them, that's what happens.*

Mostly fabricated, as it turned out. Cliff called after a few weeks to tell me that they'd finally gotten to the bottom of the situation with Vicky Gimble. She had a long history of treatment for dissociative identity disorder. He told me he didn't understand all of what they'd told him, but the gist of it was that she was crazy because one of her thought she was a person who was crazy. The other one thought she was a person who'd survived extreme gun violence, and neither acknowledged the existence of the other. It was likely that she'd experienced physical or emotional neglect or abuse as a child, but the murder-suicide was a fantasy.

None of this made me feel any better, about Vicky or about what had happened with Americans Together. Cliff intimated there might be a place for me in the back office after things settled down. I didn't ask him if he'd read my book yet. I was feeling too delicate for the answer to be no.

There were some difficult days, but eventually I realized that my departure from Americans Together had been for the best. As an operative I'd been no more than a low-level organizer, a ward heeler, and not a particularly effective one. I hated cold calls, and I hated putting the ask on people. In more than a year of serious work I'd built the Victim Alliance in our state to a grand total of nine people, two of whom were from Ryan's college and probably just felt sorry for me. After Americans Together gave me the boot, I sent emails to those nine survivors telling them that I'd moved to another position in the organization. Do you think any of them so much as wrote back? Then Biloxi happened and that frightful incident gave me some perspective.

Eight people lined up and shot, execution style, by an angry white male, in a Wendy's, of all places. After his successful suicide by cop, it came out that his former wife, who'd been dating the manager of a different fast food restaurant and who was not, by the way, present at the executions, had a restraining order against her ex. Why did he still have his gun? Heads rolled at the

Biloxi cop shop, but it was too late for the eight burger-munching innocents who, people said, had tragically been in the wrong place at the wrong time. Why did they always say that? They also said it never should have happened, and in this case I agreed with them.

State and federal law mandated that people under restraining orders should not be allowed to have guns, but even though the cops had done their job it didn't stop this clown. After they confiscated his pistols and rifles, he'd gone on the Interweb and bought him a used Ruger 9E and a buncha 17-round mags. No background check, no nothing. Then, a week before the shooting, he walked into Big Bob's Guns up in D'Iberville and purchased holster pouches and 200 rounds. Amazing, the havoc one little semi-automatic pistol could wreak. Americans Together were up in arms, so to speak, over this needless slaughter, which had been made possible by the deadly Internet Loophole.

It seemed more like a superhighway to me.

Sadly, nothing changed. The loophole bill, hastily assembled by Democrat gun grabbers, never made it out of committee. And, although the lusty cries of Americans Together dominated their Twitter and Facebook feeds, they received almost no play in the national news. Some few outsiders might have gotten the message, but odds were they already belonged to one gun control group or another. If I had any doubts before, it was now clear that my faith in advocacy had been misplaced. Governance was in the hands of unseen agents. The activists at Americans Together were merely, as Dylan had it, pawns in their game.

No, we survivors had other work to do. I had other work to do. I took another meeting at the Church of Zion with Barbara and reminded her, verbatim, of what she'd said to me—"You want to come and lend a hand, sure. We need all the help we can get." She smiled her smile and put me to work. It was a long commute from the suburbs to the slums, but with Bethany, and Ryan, and the Angels, and Hank, and my house, and my courageous memoir, and Vicky, and Americans Together, and most of the rest of what I had formerly thought of as "my life" gone, I had plenty of time on my hands.

A new $5000 donation bought me a little attention around the Church of Zion, but no real access to the Healing Collaborative. Barbara introduced me to Della, the young woman who headed the Sisters of Zion, and to the Reverend Gifford, who was in charge of programming, and to an office full of grant writers, social workers, and interns whose names I immediately forgot, and to Lonnie and his crew of social workers and first responders, a most impressive lot of serious, street-wise black dudes who looked gang hardened but talked softly, always softly. Those guys were the front end of the Healing Collaborative, and I badly wanted a piece of their action, out on the battleground, interrupting cycles of violence and turning guns into plowshares. But what use was a person of privilege to them?

I worked side-by-side with Della, Reverend Gifford, and sometimes even Barbara herself, serving meals at the nightly trauma dinners (She assured me that—simply by my presence as a caring white person—I was aiding the healing process). I gave tours of the Church and Healing Collaborative offices (mostly to other persons of privilege who were seen, without exception, as potential donors), and I started helping with *Children of Zion*, the monthly newsletter. My typing and editorial skills were much in demand.

It was my car, however, that was most highly regarded. I delivered Lonnie and the Responders to war zones in crumbling neighborhoods and carried messages and parcels to them on the doorsteps of grieving families (never to the families themselves). I listened to their accounts and complaints, rendered in laconic Ebonic, but I never got anywhere, personally, with any of them. *Children of Zion* published "My Ted Talk is Pink," and it received praise from the Reverend Gifford, as well as from the Sisters of Zion. I kept my head down and went about my work in what I hoped was a dignified manner, but I longed for the chance to show them I was more than just... whatever they seemed to think I was.

Finally, after toiling in the fields of Zion for half a year or more, an opportunity presented itself.

Februrary 9
—The Unconsidered Effects
of Black Lives Mattering

As I've indicated, the people at Americans Together felt I'd been dealt a hard blow, and I did not attempt to dissuade them. Instead, when the next Regional Victim Support Conference came up—this one was at Newton Theological Institute—I asked Mindy to use her influence to get me on the speaker's program. My topic was to be "Moving from Victim to Survivor."

I might have lost my leadership position at Americans Together, and I may have been no more than the house whitey at the Church of Zion, but I still had my story, and I still had my book. (Literally. The last 500 copies in existence were stacked in the back room of the book palace. I had no idea what a large number 500 could be until it moved in with me.) I made sure the organizers mentioned *Goodbye, My Son* in my bio in the conference program. In fact, I wrote the entry myself.

Everyone who was anyone in the gun violence prevention community showed up for the 21st Regional Victim Support Conference. It was like the Oscars. Bigwigs from Americans Together, Brady, Stop Handgun Violence, and the state Office of Victim Assistance; local pols and top cops; Barbara, Della, Reverend Gifford, and Lonnie's immaculately attired (over-dressed in their quietly dramatic way) street workers; Walter and a gaggle of his cronies from the Interfaith Council, and ladies from chapters of Americans Together. And those were only the ones I recognized. The bulk of the audience, about 200 of them, were professional service providers and victim advocates, public and private, from three states. The cream of the crop.

The organizers had given me fifteen minutes right at the top of the program, after the keynote speaker—young Senator Perkins, of all people—who was seen by everyone giving me a sympathetic man hug. True, I was just the opening act for the Harvard Professor whose metrics destroyed all the NRA myths about good guys with guns, but I was excited about my debut. I was determined to do Dennis Sykes proud as a motivational speaker. Although, of course, there could be no way he'd ever know.

I was a big fan of the MacArthur genius Robert Sapolsky. In the seclusion of the book palace, I'd watched hours of his YouTube talks on biology and human behavior, and I sought to replicate his jaunty, offhanded manner of presenting startling insights as he paced up and down the stage behind the podium.

I practiced and practiced until my own movements up and down the ten feet blocked out in front of Hank's desk synchronized with my scripted speech:

"... Anyway, there's this whole thing about Breast Cancer Awareness that the gun violence movement doesn't yet have." *pause, turn*

"I mean, breast cancer AWARENESS? Really?" *walking slowly downstage*

"Is there anyone in America who's not aware of breast cancer? Who wouldn't know where to go if they needed more information?" *pause, turn toward audience*

"Pink isn't about raising awareness. It's about AFFIRMING awareness." *arrive at the podium for the punch line*

"We'll never solve the problems of gun violence until we, as a nation, face the fact that gun violence is a problem."

The fifteen minutes I'd been so worried about filling seemed more like three minutes as I paced up and down the stage, rolling out the story of how Richard Winters's criminal trial had turned me from a helpless victim into a reporter—a person with agency, someone who could do something about his situation, as I had done in *Goodbye, My Son* (a copy of which I plucked off the podium upon my arrival there from downstage, and waved dramatically in the air). We couldn't all be writers, I told them, but we were more than helpless victims. We were survivors. And they called us survivors because we had survived.

Basking in the afterglow of my performance, feeling the sweat cool as I sat in the front row with the other speakers while the Harvard Professor held forth, I suddenly experienced the faintest intrusion of uncertainty, as if the fellow next to me had shifted his elbow a bit, the way an airplane seatmate might, and had brushed, not jabbed, my rib.

Bar graphs and pie charts lit the screen behind the Harvard Professor. "Not only does owning a gun not make you safer, you are much more likely to die from a gun if you own one..."

No, it *was* a jab. A sharp poke. Compared to the welcome the audience had given the Harvard Professor as he walked to the podium, the applause I received as I'd exited the stage had been tepid. My performance-generated adrenalin began to metabolize and was replaced, not by the calm certainty of a job well done, but by a pang roughly equivalent to the sensation that might arise from having a ballpoint pen jammed into my chest, right at the top of my modest pot belly, just below the heart. It dawned on me that the audience hadn't laughed at a single one of the jokes I'd carefully and considerately built in. My efforts had gotten no reaction from that mob of social workers and shrinks. Absolute zero.

"Nearly every gun that is used to hurt someone, anyone, started out as the property of a legal gun owner," the Harvard Professor said.

It had been in the first few minutes of my talk, as I was running through the foundational annual numbers—40,000 gun deaths, two-thirds of them suicides, leaving about 10,000 gun murders, "And 1000 people shot by cops." *pause, turn,* "You know. The gang-bangers. Guys who deserve to be shot by cops, that sort of thing."

As I spoke those words, and began my slow walk to the other end of the stage, I saw Lonnie's gang of street workers look at one another in astonishment. Then, before I could deliver my next line, they rose as one and walked out of the auditorium. *Must've gotten a call,* I told myself. But even before I'd reached the far end of the platform I knew but could not at that moment admit that I knew.

Black lives mattered.

In my bland assumption that those thousand people (let's face it—mostly young African-American males) who had been murdered by cops somehow deserved what they got, I stood revealed as just another uneducated bigot.

Can you feel my anguish? The Harvard Professor sat down to thunderous applause and when the lady from Grannies Against Guns got up to do her bit I made for the men's room. The eyes that followed me up the aisle could have been the eyes of sailors watching Jonah cross the deck. My talk had been a failure. Worse than a failure. It had been a stink bomb. A stinky stink bomb. I vomited into a toilet in a stinky stall, washed my face, dried my tears, and made my brave re-entry (I was ignored) into the auditorium in time for the presentation on social media and teen suicide. I'd embarrassed myself, shat myself, wet my pants in public, in front of my peers and colleagues. *Black lives mattered.* And in one unfortunate, tone-deaf turn of phrase about guys who "deserved to be shot by cops" I destroyed whatever credibility I'd managed to accrue with the very people I so desperately wished to join.

That sting was sharp because it stung my ego. But worse—sneakily worse—was the larger truth I discovered lying coiled in the Book Palace upon my return (I'd fled the conference at lunch break). Not only had my talk been a failure, my very existence as someone who had transcended victimization by his own devices was unacceptable. Anathema. Those people in the audience, those care givers and therapists and nurses and shrinks, made their livings helping victims. Anyone who could help himself was a threat to them. No wonder they hadn't laughed at my jokes. There was nothing funny about me. They needed to see a genuine, fully-flayed victim. All they got was a wannabe Sapolsky honkie.

After a while I received a letter from Barbara asking what had become of me? But I never wrote back. I was too busy dealing with the painful realization that I had no place in her church. No place in her world.

February 10
—The Big Hurt

The hurt hurt worse after my revelation about Americans Together.

I'd always understood that one of their primary functions—along with making noise about the insane proliferation of guns in our society—was the creation of the National Victim Database. Polls and statistics told us that almost 60% of Americans had been affected in some way by gun violence. That was a substantial majority in the contemporary political world, and Americans Together was assembling a database of those people, of that majority, so that when the crucial time arrived, they could press a button and the hundreds of millions of survivor-citizens in the National Victim Database would rise as one to overthrow those bastards at the NRA, and their political toadies.

That was what they told me, and that was what I believed as I struggled to enter my measly collection of survivor information into the database.

Then, shortly after the mess with Vicky, I began receiving email solicitations from other gun violence prevention organizations and groups that supported parents of murdered children. Then from life insurance companies, then a barrage of ads from travel agencies, cellphone networks, fast food chains, bargain clothing outlets and other Internet lice.

I was too distracted by my work at the Church of Zion to pay those ads much mind, but in the desolation that followed my failure at the Victim Support Conference, the ugly truth bubbled up before my eyes. Americans Together was raising money by selling personal information from the National Victim Database to other organizations and companies. By selling *my* personal information. Despicable, when you think about it that way. The whole thing was a scam, and my noble colleagues in the struggle against gun violence were nothing but lousy scammers. As Andy Willets had suggested, they were probably working hand-in-glove with the pro-gun crowd.

Just a moment ago I stepped outside the Book Palace and the stars were ablaze in the wintry sky. No moon. I watched them crackle and dance, thinking how I used to be able to recognize the constellations they formed. When had I lost the knack of seeing them that way? There used to be hunters and swans and chariots. Tonight, they were a jumble. The same but different. That was how I felt for months after parting ways with Barbara and losing my faith in Americans Together.

Only gradually did I become aware that the world around me was constellating itself anew. The pains I experienced were growth pains. I hadn't been cast out. I'd been liberated.

The thing our true rulers— those unseen masters of governance—don't understand—haven't even considered (just like the teenage suicide videos, which only *seemed* to stop after Facebook developed an algorithm to take them down more efficiently, but in reality are replicating themselves continually on channels known only to potential teen suicides)—is that once people see why the murders happened, they'll happen again. They will. And again.

When Chester Himes learned of the acquittal of the white men who'd tortured and lynched Emmett Till (for supposedly whistling at a white woman) he said, "The real horror comes when your dead brain must face the fact that we as a nation don't want it to stop. If we wanted to, we would."

People will realize that they need to keep killing the people responsible for the killings, until people understand—their dead brains register the fact—that if they want it to stop, they can stop it.

Americans Together is sending me car ads now. (Flash of National Victim Database spiders crawling through the System; the teeny, sharp feet of spiders seeking cracks.)

I need to back up here just a scooch, as Vicky used to say. The details of my personal development have been pouring forth with such insistence that I've omitted important broader topics relating to my discovery of the underlying causes of America's gun sickness, and the manner in which inoculation by gun is bound to effect its ultimate cure. Grand sounding phrases, I know. It's the whiskey talking.

The whiskey conversing with the pills, cooking up circuitous locutions, conjuring ways of avoiding Barbara's simple question: *How did it get to murder?* I think Chester Himes was living in Paris then. Paris would be good.

My comprehension of the awful truth began with a couple of mosquitoes. The inspiration for its awfuller consequences originated in a simple charitable act, performed almost unconsciously, when I was first working for Americans Together. I'd forgotten all about that. But Nadine Hampton had not.

After our round table fact-finding session with the politicians had ended, and after those volcanic mothers of murdered sons, as well as the more demure ladies from the suburbs, had posed for pictures with Senator Perkins and Representatives Hart and Crowley, each on her iPhone, taken by someone else, bound within seconds for Facebook, Twitter, Instagram, Pinterest, Snapchat, Tik Tok, and a dozen other social media platforms—as we trooped through the impressive tropical atrium at Harborside Hotel, I felt a hand grasp my elbow and turned to see Nadine.

She was a large woman with tattoos on her shoulders and gold hoops in her ears. Somewhat taken aback, I told her, "You were very powerful in there. All of you."

"You don't remember me, do you?"

"I didn't at first, but as soon as you started to talk I recognized you."

"We got a check from you. It was for $500."

"That's right."

"And you sent a note. You said you wanted to get together sometime and talk about the things you and Americans Together could do to help the Enduring Memory Sisters. Do you remember that?"

"I do now, yes."

"And I sent you a thank-you note, but we never did get together."

"You're busy. I understand."

"But I do want to talk with you because..." By this time our crowd had reached the revolving doors at the front of the atrium. She moved us out of the stream of traffic. "Because I heard what the Senators said in there about how complicated gun violence is, and how deep it runs. It runs deep, all right, like a virus in the body. But it's not complicated. You got to understand that. Otherwise you're just going round in circles like them. When somebody gets shot and killed in our neighborhood the first thing we want to know is how did the gun get there? Somebody put it in that kid's hand. Sometimes it's his girlfriend. You know what a Ride or Die chick is, right?"

I had no idea.

She said, "We spend a lot of time working with young ladies trying to get them to understand that if their man gets busted with a gun in his car, they're the ones gonna do the time, because they made the buy for him. Or sometimes a guy will come up from South Carolina or wherever with a trunk full of them and be selling them right on the street. That's why we want to know where did it come from, how did it get here? You stop the gun, and you stop a killing. Simple as that."

Nadine's intensity compressed the moment into a

dot. She looked like Queequeg. Her hands came toward me. I extended my right hand reflexively. She grasped it in both of hers. They were white inside. As the last of the Enduring Memory Sisters passed us by, she said, "All you got to do is follow the money."

I stood there, bewildered, as Nadine's tattoos and gold hoops slid through the revolving door. Follow the money? What was I supposed to make of that?

But it stuck, like a bit of dinner between my teeth, and I worked it the way you'd work the bothersome morsel, attempting to dislodge it until, at the far end of the money trail, the triumvirate snapped into place. Freedman made the stuff, Becker did the marketing, and Sawtelle facilitated it all. I could *see* the infernal machine, grinding away in the void before me. Chewing us up. Spitting us out. Over and over. Almost as if I were praying.

But I hadn't yet figured out what to do about it. I was still in the process of digesting the information, of moving the puzzle pieces around to see how they fit.

Anyway, the Richard Winters prison visitation scheme was taking up most of my attention. My hopes for finding a place in the hearts of the American people were pinned on the poignant meeting of Richard and Joe. Americans wanted Forgiveness? We'd give them some! It would be my ultimate performance, our mutual redemption, enacted in the name of every survivor of gun violence, of everyone who'd suffered what I had suffered. The project loomed large. So large that I wasn't ready to tackle it.

Fortunately, perhaps wisely, I'd become more involved in the book trade following Hank's departure. I spent countless hours in front of the computer, uploading fresh stock to online sales venues. The screen's blue light cooled me, calmed me, spared me the pain of dwelling on my losses. Or it enabled me to transfer personal losses to business losses. I'd developed quite a knack for that.

Despite my intensified efforts, the new listings refused to generate better sales numbers. My objects of desire continued to languish—by this time there were 3823 of them, with an aggregate retail value of more than $2.5 million. What was *wrong* with people? Then I woke up one morning and cut the prices of all my online listings by a third. With these fancy databases you can do that just by pushing a button. The price of the journal of the mad whaling captain that I'd bought from Andy plummeted from $7500 to $5000. Soon thereafter I got a call from a big institutional library in Virginia. They wanted to add the journal to their collection of American manuscripts, but it was the end of their current budget cycle and funds were low. Could I do any better on the price? I sold it to them for $4500. I'd paid $5500 for it, but that was then. This was now and I needed the $4500.

Actually, I didn't need the money at all. My share from the sale of the house had been in excess of $350,000. What I needed was some activity to balance my increasing fixation on the gun industry. I could hear group-trainer Danutia over my shoulder, breathing good air in, bad air out. What did she mean by that? What did it mean that when air got inside you it turned bad? Could a person breathe good air out? Would that be a bad thing? Then it was time to go down to Florida for the annual Rare Book and Manuscript Librarian's Conference.

Philadelphia, Las Vegas, San Diego, Baton Rouge—every year the Rare Book Librarians held their conference in a different city. Professional book and manuscript curators from all over America got together to schmooze, and a number of specialized antiquarian book dealers were invited to the bivouac. Because of the kind of material in which I dealt (things that don't exist, in case you've forgotten), I'd been attending these conferences for years. The current iteration was in Miami, so I flew down there for a week of sunshine, back slapping, and good air.

But Florida... Florida!

It didn't dawn on me until I was squeezing into my seat on that miserable American Airlines cattle jet. Florida was right up there with Texas and a few other states when it came to gun idiocy. As soon as I got to my hotel room, I consulted my smartphone and found three shooting ranges in the immediate vicinity. The one called Lock 'n Load had what I was looking for.

According to its website, and the cheery Tommy Gun logo painted on the front of the white cinder-block building, it offered the public "The Full Auto Experience"—a smorgasbord of fully automatic weapons available for civilians to play with. It wasn't cheap; my two hours there cost me nearly $500. But by the time I was finished, I had the satisfaction of having handled those formidable weapons. Of having made their acquaintance, of having mastered them. A satisfaction fathers of children murdered by semi-automatic rifles were not supposed to experience, let alone enjoy.

For my full-auto joy ride, I selected three "assault rifles" that ascended the evolutionary chain—from the primitive AK47 (Automat Kalashnikov, 1947), to the standard U.S. Military M4 carbine, to the Heckler-Koch 417, a fine piece of machinery engineered in Austria. Not surprisingly, the AK47 was stinky and slow, with lots of kickback. The M4 was a little better, but I still couldn't imagine actually aiming it and hitting a target on full auto. Firing the HK 417, by contrast, was like driving a BMW. A novel experience, to be sure, but by the time I'd blatted out a few hundred rounds, the whole thing began to bore me. Too much noise and smoke. Too little control. I was stuck with a persistent image of sausage grinders, God knows why, and a feeling of disdain. I much preferred the manner in which my little pistol and I sought the bullseye.

In the instruction room, while a serious, buff young instructor named Rick (no Bubbas at Lock 'n Load!) taught me about the gun I'd be shooting next, I could hear the "pop, pop, pop... braaat" of the other clients' rifles being fired. At one point my instruction was punctuated by a different noise, a deep thud, like a detonation. I asked Rick what had caused it.

"You ever see *American Sniper*?"

The .50 caliber American Sniper Experience cost $15 a round, and it was worth every penny. The bullet was as big as a carrot. With rangefinder and ballistic calculator properly sighted in, Rick assured me, those babies could take out a man a mile away.

After that experience, the Rare Book and Manuscript Librarian's Conference seemed a little, oh, I don't know. Bland, I guess. Although I did get to talk with the guy from the big library in Virginia about the mad whaling captain's journal. It seemed their department had undergone an audit recently, and the check would be a month or two late arriving. I didn't mind, did I?

There was no putting it off any longer. I made ready to sit down, in the guise of another man, with Ryan's killer. Calm and perfectly empty, as I said, having been given an emotional enema by my soon-to-be ex-wife.

I knew, going in, that it would not be possible to have that already impossible conversation with Richard Winters. I mean the conversation about what he did and why he did it. I mean the impossibility of apology, and the Vanity of forgiveness. Utterly impossible. This made my scheme for our anti-gun commercial shine even more brilliantly in my eyes. Instead of attempting to traverse the soggy barrens of loss and guilt, I'd keep to higher ground. Under my guidance, we'd discuss ways in which we might use our shared story to create a powerful message about gun violence. Playing on his narcissism, I'd propose that we create a Public Service Announcement. An anti-gun commercial starring him!

We'd write it together and somehow I'd get a video of him saying his lines. A news crew on Media Day? I'd find a way to get it done, and I'd find a film editor to help me, and we'd hone it down to a short piece, and we'd put it on You Tube. Hollywood liberals would pick it up and it would go viral! Not candles, tears, and impassioned slogans, but rough and edgy, like those anti-tobacco ones in which the skeletal cancer patient says, *This is the reality, and it sucks. Don't smoke.* Except that Richard would be saying his piece from a prison cell. I was on fire with the idea. I'd pitch it to the murderer of my son, and we'd talk about it. The resulting conversation would be interesting and constructive, vastly more productive than the impossible, *Why did you do it, Richard? Or, How could such a thing have happened?*—The very question I'd addressed years before on innumerable talk shows, Richard Winters would now answer. *Because it's so easy for people to get guns, that's how!*

I went on the Department of Correction website and downloaded the thirty-six-page document that detailed the rules and regulations for visiting inmates. I also reviewed the procedure for visitation in Richard's prison. The process was straightforward. I show up on a day scheduled for visits. I take a number, fill out a form, produce ID. They call my number and I get searched. Waistband and shoes. I am forbidden to wear jeans, other clothing resembling prison garb, clothing with gang insignia, or any of another half page of dress code restrictions that would not in a million years apply to a privileged suburban dresser like myself. I enter the pedestrian trap, a secure closet with locked doors fore and aft, then go down a walk leading to the visitation room, where my papers are checked once again, after which I am let into a community room equipped with vending machines and chairs.

And there he sat. So unlike what I'd anticipated that the first sight of him knocked the wind out of me. No longer the skinny geek of the criminal trial. I saw broad shoulders beneath Richard's blue prison shirt and sparkling white undershirt. A man's body. Ryan would have a man's body by now, too. Not even that he *should,* just that he would. Time was roaring along too fast for me to catch up. Clear eyes, brownish green, placid.

He rose. A little taller than me, just a trace of a belly.

Big, soft hands, soft grip.

"Hello, mister Mooney."

"Richard..." His eyes.

"You know I'd trade places with your son if I could."

A moment of horror, as I encountered the deadly bog I'd been so desperate to steer clear of—that somehow I had exchanged Ryan for him.

It must have showed on my face because he immediately added, "In the grave. If I could, I'd give my life for any of the people I killed. I want you to know that."

The horror gave way to panic. Thirty seconds in,

and this conversation had already run off the rails. "I don't know what to say."

"You don't have to say anything, mister Mooney. I know you and missus Mooney hate me. I don't want to change that. You have good reason to hate me." Prison had worn away most of his accent. His voice had deepened since the night of that infamous 911 call. *I just shot some people at Brier Hill College.*

"Would you like a Coke or something?"

"We're not allowed to use the vending machines."

"That's all right. I bought a debit card out front." Robots, where are you?

"When I got that letter from you telling me that I'd be getting an important visit from a man named Jim Farrell, I knew exactly what you were doing. Don't ask me how."

Was that solid ground under my feet? "I've got an idea, Richard. A plan, really. And I needed to talk to you about it in person. It's something we have to work on together. Something that will help us get our message out."

Once we were on my script, working together on our script, things moved right along. Richard was calm, solicitous, and intelligent. A smart kid or, I should say, a smart young man. As I'd hoped, he liked my idea for a PSA. He reminded me that a crew of Germans had filmed an interview with him for a documentary about American mass murderers—a topic of endless fascination to Germans. Did I remember that he'd assented to the interview provided they contributed $5000 to the Ryan fund? Ah, of course! Contrary to the information provided by Ms. Bull Connors of the Department of Correction, there was a standard procedure for access to inmates for documentary or educational purposes. He was certain that we could find a way to do what the Germans had done.

Then he went quiet for a minute. It wasn't a sulk; he was thinking. I sat there, catching my emotional breath, while he did what he needed to do.

Presently he said, "Mister Mooney, we should both be in this commercial. We could film me here in prison, and you at a studio or in your house. Then cut them in together, edit them. You come on first and say who you are and what happened. Then I come on and say who I am and what I did. Then I say, 'When I was so disturbed I thought God was talking to me, it was still a simple matter for me to walk into a store and buy a gun.' How much screen time would that take?"

"Jeez, Richard. That's terrific!"

We timed the lines by the clock on the wall above the soda machine.

"Forty seconds. We need less or more."

"Well," he said. "It can't be less. How about you come on again and close the piece out by telling the people to vote for background checks?"

"I'll say, 'It's too late for Ryan, and it's too late for Richard, but it's not too late for you.' Looking right out there at them. Then we could put any message in there, really. Waiting periods, background checks, magazine-size limits, any of that."

"Or, how about this? How about you say the 'too late' part and then I come on at the very end and say, 'But it's not too late for you,' looking right at the people."

With the extra lines it took almost two minutes. Richard ending, "But it's not too late for you." Looking dead into the hypothetical camera with those eyes, the things they'd seen! Then a final closeup of my ravaged visage. A splendid piece of work for two tortured souls finding redemption through a Public Service Announcement. Richard seemed as excited by the idea as I was, and I began to let myself hope that this wild thing might actually find its way into your living room.

We fiddled with the idea a bit more, then there was nothing left but small talk. I asked after Billy and

Doreen. He told me that his mom had had a cancer scare, but that it had turned out okay. He asked about Bethany (He referred to her as missus and me as mister, which I let stand). I told him she was doing great, that she was going back to college to become a speech therapist. I told him I was working for Americans Together Against Gun Violence and for the Trauma Center at the Church of Zion. I told him I worked with survivors and that I gave workshops and lectures about transcending victimization. I told him I had written articles and was working on another book. I told him Spike Lee might help us with our PSA. I told him a lot of things, but finally there were no more lies to divert or further forestall the moment that must, inevitably, impossibly, arrive.

He said, "I know you want to know what happened that night."

Did I? Not from him. I already knew what had happened that night. It had taken all these difficult years to work my way out of the moment of Ryan's death, him lying on the sidewalk leaking blood, gasping, "I'm dying" with kids screaming all around him, going out of their minds watching one of their own take his last breath. Jolting awake even these nights wondering if he'd been thinking of his girlfriend—his first true love—as he died? His mom? Was he thinking of me? How much of it was pain and what sort of pain? What sort of agony knowing in those last moments that his life had been stolen? What could Richard have told me about any of that? And yet... I couldn't speak. He continued.

"You know those guys I hung around with? The three guys you wrote about?"

Richard had been part of a little clique of outcasts who seemed to savor their rejection, behaving as politically incorrectly as they could in that hotbed of political correctness. Making racist comments, giving one another the Nazi salute, terrorizing female students. One of the most damning things about the college administrators was that they'd failed to act on the many complaints against these four young terrorists. The Dean of Students, that dope, cited freedom of speech— an error in judgment on the same level of incompetence as refusing to believe that Richard Winters had a gun.

"These guys," he was saying, "They were—*we* were—into some weird stuff. It started out as a protest, you know, against that self-righteous enlightened culture everyone worshiped. Like it was a dress code. That was why we all had Marine-style haircuts and wore conservative clothes. And listened to Fox News and programs like that in the TV room at the dorm. It started out as a goof, but then we really got into it, though we didn't have any idea what we were doing. We just had a romance with the hollowness of everything around us." He surveyed the room. "You know, the material world, the atoms and molecules of it are mostly empty space (Oh, I knew!). The empty things people say and do. The bullshit. Politicians, parents, teachers, the other kids. It was just a void. But there was nothing to replace it with except... nothing."

"Voices?" I croaked, "Did you ever hear voices?"

He shook his head. "No voices. None of that stuff they said at the trial was true. It was something else, something we were chasing, then courting, the four of us. We didn't drink or do drugs. We spent a lot of time in the weight room. We lived clean because it was the opposite of what everyone else was doing. But I felt this powerful thing. We all did. And it was almost as if we could summon it, feed it, romance it."

There was a terrible roaring noise, but I was above it, looking down on that Texas-sized swirl in the Pacific Ocean. Richard kept talking, telling me things about this nothing of his. My throat hurt. I wished I'd gotten a Coke. He never blinked. Jim Farrell should have been sitting there, not me.

Richard was saying, "We called it to us. It gave us power. I didn't tell any of my crew about the gun. The whole thing was supposed to be a surprise. But if I hadn't done it, one of the others would have."

Dr. Rodgers, the shrink who'd examined Richard, had told me something else when I asked him if he thought Richard was conning me. He told me that, in the old days, before the *Diagnostic and Statistical Manual*, there were more informal, anecdotal ways of making diagnoses. He said it was commonly understood that, when you spoke with a true psychopath, the hair on the back of your neck would stand up. He told me that the first time he interviewed Richard after the shootings, the hair on the back of his neck stood up.

I told Richard, "I think we'd better end this now."

Richard just sat there, watching me.

In the parking lot I felt nothing so much as relief at being out from under the maleficent thumb of the Department of Correction. You don't realize it while you're in there because the environment is so strange and new, but once you get outside you can feel it lifting, that sense of them being constantly *on* you, and it feels good.

So good, in fact, that it nearly offset my anger at having been tricked by that miserable son of a bitch in there and his—had he actually used the word *vortex* on me, or had I just imagined it? Pretending to be listening to me, playing along with my fantasy, then dropping that bomb. That was what he was doing, wasn't it? Toying with me, tormenting me? "If I hadn't done it, one of the others would have." What else could that be but a reenactment, in my presence, of the murder of my son?

There were so many things I didn't want to think about just then! In truth, I left that place in a panic, rushing out the door as if there'd been a fire inside. On fire inside. Totally unprepared, running smack into the fact that the idea of Bethany emptying me had been nonsense. She had nothing to do with what I'd experienced in there. What had I experienced in there? It had been idiotic to just barge in and sit down with him. That Connors lady had been right. That was why they had special people, "victim-offender dialogue facilitators," (I looked into the matter later, once it was too late, of course), to guide you through the process. It was not something one did on one's own. Like giving a loaded gun to a three-year-old. No, not like that at all. What the hell was I doing to myself?

I hunkered down in the Book Palace, waiting for the gift of healing to kick in. Waiting in vain, it seemed. A suitcase in my hand.

Into this mess waded Andy Willets, dangling another object of desire in front of me. It was a manuscript entitled *Tagliches Gesang-Buchlein*—"Daily Song Book"—a devotional guide, containing about 350 pages of hymns, prayers and songs, hand written, in immaculate German fraktur script, sometime in the early 1700s by a female disciple of the Schwenkfelders, a German-American religious community outside of Philadelphia. The paper bore the William Rittenhouse water-mark, from the mill that produced the first paper made in America. The binding was full calf with brass clasps and corners. Brilliant workmanship, entirely American, contemporaneous with the paper; it was probably, judging from the rope-braid tooling beneath the bands, done by Balthasar Hoffman, an 18th Century book binder who lived and worked in proximity to the Rittenhouse paper mill. That was what Andy told me, anyway, and it sounded legit.

This time we met at a diner off Route 84, just north of Hartford, Connecticut. Andy was on his way to Ohio for the Springfield Antique Show and Flea Market, and I was on the Road to Nowhere, as the Talking Heads would say. Unlike the deplorable Cracker Barrel, this place served alcohol, and most of the clientele seemed on the good side of type 2 diabetes. I ordered a beer, a Greek salad, and the open turkey sandwich. Andy had a Manhattan on the rocks and the Yankee pot roast, which was on special that day.

I held the little book in my hands and it positively glowed. The way whatever was inside that suitcase in the movie *Pulp Fiction* glowed. You never saw the stuff itself, just the glow. People died for that glow, and I would have killed for the *Tagliches Gesang-Buchlein*— in a manner of speaking, of course. Instead, I wrote Andy a check for $10,000. Which was really only $5500 if you subtracted the payment for the mad whaling captain's journal, which I did, in my mental cash flow accounting, even though the people at the library in Virginia hadn't paid me yet. It was the end of their fiscal year or something.

Our deal was done before the waitress even came back with the food. The book sat beside me in the booth, snuggled back up in bubble wrap inside double plastic bags to protect it from flying pot roast particles. Drinks were renewed and the salads arrived. I had no desire for dinnertime small talk about the price of gas or some similar inanity. I needed to tell him what I'd done, what had happened to me since our last, fateful conversation, how my brilliant idea for a gun commercial had blown up in my face.

"I got a gun," I said. "A 9 mm carry gun. I've also schooled myself in the operation of the AR platform, and have experience shooting an AK47, an M4 carbine, an HK 417, and the Fifty Light and M24 sniper rifles. Now, when I give testimony about gun violence, I tell people I'm a Marine Corps veteran, a licensed gun owner, and the father of a boy killed in a school shooting. That really gets their attention." I hadn't done any testifying, because no one had called on me to testify about anything since the round table session with Nadine and the politicians. But if anyone ever called on me again, I was sure that intro would be a big hit. The acquisition of the *Tagliches Gesang-Buchlein* had pumped me up like an inflatable sex doll.

"What does owning a gun have to do with reducing gun violence?"

"I posed as another man," I told him. "I found a guy who looked like me and I used his ID to get into the prison where they keep Ryan's killer."

"They'd never let you smuggle a gun into prison. And anyway, what does owning a gun have to do with reducing gun violence?"

"The gun has nothing to do with it. I just wanted to talk to him."

Andy looked around the room, at the ceiling, out the door. "That's pretty darned weird, Joe... Hey, can you believe gas is down to $3.25? They're giving the stuff away! Pretty soon it'll be cheaper than water."

Really? Was that all I'd wanted to do? Just talk to Richard Winters? About what, if not Ryan's murder? The ineffable *why?* The inflatable *why?* Whys like stars in milky ways. Swirling oceans of whys preceding a trigger pull. Whys to drown in.

Was it the toilet swirl of my hopeless infatuation with that little *Tagliches Gesang-Buchlein?* I'll never know. No sooner had I summoned up my aborted prison visit than the vision of that vortex came back to me, redoubled. I could see it swirling and hovering, circling the globe, feeding on human misery each time it descended. I could imagine it enveloping the Chicken Plant shooter, just as it had enveloped Richard Winters. It would always select the weakest, the most broken, to do its bidding. Just add the gun and you get Lee Harvey Oswald, Charles Whitman; you know the way

Andy's yakking form went in and out, black and white. My little *Buchlein* and I tumbled deeper into the vortex. No, not so much falling as impelled inward, pushing deeper to penetrate its core, driven by the same impulse that inspired the investigation that became *Goodbye, My Son*. I hadn't written that book in order to reach out to other people. I wrote it for myself and for Ryan, to explore the nature of an evil that had crossed our paths. I felt like a weather plane flying into a hurricane. If Richard was crazy, how could he be blamed? No way to go but through it. We'd make a commercial against guns and put it on YouTube. It would go bacterial! Infectious puss bombs exploding in America's face. Was it Vanity to think I could convince the American public of anything? My ego jolted though bands swirling around the storm's eye. Mindy's hand upon the table at the Irish bar. Nadine's white palms. I was back on my pony, tracking the bastards who did this to us. Nadine and me, and each of those ladies at the round table, and Barbara and Dennis! And my poor, dear Bethany, gone off to some Cape. And what about those Bouncy Castle parents?

Now I understood the knuckleheads in the Texas legislature, and every poor deluded soul who believed God had given him the right to walk around with a gun. Followers of Christ Jesus whose homes were armories. Brigades of ignorant, arrogant, innocent pawns. Survivalists, Hunter Thompson replicants, video game addicts, conspiracy theorists spewing paranoid reflux. Gun control won't work for them.

Not only will it not work, it's a bad idea in a country where no one is safe and the police are, by definition, always late, where we're all ripe targets for muggings, rapes, and home invasions perpetrated by crack heads, thugs, and angry black jailbirds. If they know we're carrying guns they'll stay away from us. They'll use their guns on one another. It makes intuitive sense.

Crazy fanatics who have penetrated every level of our society, prowling the country searching out gun-free zones in which to carry out their slaughter orgies without interference. There's no way to stop them, but we can limit the damage they cause by being armed and vigilant at all times—particularly during church services, while attending school, while hanging out in shopping malls, and when using public transportation. A terrible shame, but that's the way things are.

Yet people want to outlaw guns, despite knowing full well that if you outlaw guns, only outlaws will have guns. Gun laws turn law-abiding Americans into sheep waiting to have their throats ripped open by dangerous predators; gun laws will lead to a law-abider genocide, since it is a well-known historical fact that the first thing the Nazis did before they gassed the Jews was to register and then confiscate their assault rifles.

Is that what we want in this country? Do we want millions of gun-owning good guys gassed in ovens? Do we want to have our throats torn open? Because that's what will happen, make no mistake. And then it will just be the predators, and they'll own all the guns, and we sheep won't have any freedom because we'll be dead. Is that what we want?

Guns to keep us safe from guns. Pistols on night tables, in handbags, under shirts in the shirt drawer, suspended from belts encircling paunches, waiting. Flowing up the Iron Pipeline into the hands of untrained nitwits, potential suicides, and kids with still-developing brains. "Modern Sporting Rifles."

Baboon politicians bent over, sucking themselves off, assholes raised for NRA dicks. Gun companies under the protection of Congress pumping death into American society. *How could such a terrible thing have happened?* Look the other way, my friend.

Look the other way when that poor woman, on her sight-seeing tour through the American criminal justice system, opens the crime-scene triptych of her daughter's corpse. Look the other way when duplicitous glad-handers in thousand-dollar suits vote down commonsense gun laws. Look the other way when congressional stooges conspire with the gun industry to stoke hatred and fear in their benighted constituents, selling them guns to protect some misbegotten idea of Freedom. Can anyone truly believe jackbooted government thugs are coming to invade each household in America, to confiscate 400 million guns? They'd have to raise another Army, and they can't get enough men or money for the Army they've already got. What kind of dupe could ever entertain such a stupid idea?

How could a person so lose touch with the idea of a decent life?

Sunshine was leaking through the dusty window into the back room of the Book Palace. Somehow, I'd gotten into my cot and had slept the sleep of the dead because, unusually for me, I had no recollection of any dream, just lingering vortices. Now someone was pounding on the door. I crawled out from the burrow I'd made in the covers and discovered that I had all my clothes on. Must've been quite a night! I padded through the front room, *All right already!* threw the front door open, and there was Ryan.

Ryan and Bethany. And Hank, and Hallie, and Rachel, and Mindy, and Barbara, and Andy, and Doreen and Billy, and Vicky. Like Christmas carolers. Boughs of kindly evergreens everywhere.

"What in God's name are you all doing here?"

Ryan said, "It's time to wake up, Pops." Dark pools of eyes to drown in. I began to weep.

APRIL 3

I haven't been well. An insidious flu-like malaise, non-Covidian, mental and physical, very like the illness that came upon me last summer.

Following my calamitous prison interview with Richard, I began having terrible headaches, accompanied by pits of depression so steep I couldn't climb out, alternating with fits of anger at the bastards who did this to us, so concentrated and clear as to border on ecstasy. Beginning with the infernal machine grinding away out there in the void, and those unseen lever-pulling hands, but leaking quickly down to gun industry tycoons, the NRA and their lobbyists, greedy financiers, racists, climate change deniers, drivers who refused to use their turn signals, and losers who didn't have their money ready at the supermarket checkout counter. Like trying to carry spring water in my hands. Like Ryan's blood.

And what were my prospects? Summer was approaching, my favorite season. But all too soon the long, generous days would pass in their usual tragic manner. We'd be headed for the dark time again, the season of Ryan's death, and I'd be headed for trouble. I made a vow to myself that if things didn't improve by

Labor Day, I'd give Walter a call and ask him to get me some help. A spin-dry cycle in rehab, maybe. Maybe a semester at some posh loony bin. Or maybe he kept straitjackets at the church. It was a dire situation, and yet some part of me remained intact.

I went to our family Doc and told him I was having trouble sleeping. He gave me a scrip for zolpidem—wonderful stuff. A few whiskeys and a couple of pills, and it was Good Night, Irene. Usually, I'd wake refreshed. If not, I'd hold out as long as I could then repeat. For the headaches there was always oxycodone. At $50 for one little 50M pill it was highway robbery, but these were extraordinary circumstances. Anyway, I had the dough, and now I had a plan. I knew my pills, and I knew I wasn't going to get hooked on anything in a mere six weeks of abuse. Does it even qualify as abuse if it's part of a carefully conceived regimen? Self-conceived, and self-administered, I admit, but still.

Cycleswithincycles,wheelswithinwheels.Incontrast to the bad days, the good ones seemed good indeed. There was, suddenly, so much to do! The cleanness of my rage tipped me back toward functionality. I sang my *Taglisches Gesang* to the Huntington Museum out in California, and the manuscript librarian at that august institution fell in love with my precious *Buchlein*, just as I had. She promised to pitch it in the most glowing terms to her superiors, and I sent it to her on approval.

It had never been my desire to *own* those objects of desire. My thrill was in acquiring them, in the hunt, in the research, in the final, triumphant description. Definitely something sexual about it; I'm thinking of Fowles's *The Collector*. But as Miles Davis would say, *So What?* When I heard the excitement in that librarian's voice I felt as if a circuit had been closed. I'd identified a rare and precious cultural commodity. I'd rescued it from a yard sale, a trash can, or some similarly inglorious fate—well, actually, Andy had, but he couldn't have done it without my 10 Gs behind him—and I delivered it to a place that would put it to its best and highest use. Andy could never have done that part of it. I didn't feel bad when it was gone. I felt great.

I crashed soon after, which was to be expected. Whiskey and pills, and within a week I was back on my bike, touring the neighborhood, breathing in the sweet summer air. *Hi mister Farrell!* I made an outline of my redemption memoir (with the vortex omitted from the prison scene) and sent it to Daniel who, to my astonishment, returned my email.

Writer's joke. Two writers meet on the street.

Writer 1: Hey Sam! How's it going?

Writer 2: Well, my house burned down and I lost my dog and all my possessions.

Writer 1: Oh, that's terrible

Writer 2: But my agent called!

Okay, I was never any good at canned jokes. He told me I was on to something, but that I needed to go into more detail about the dissolution of my marriage. "This isn't just about you," he said. "People will want to know about Bethany and how Ryan's death affected her."

That sent me down again. What could I say about the dissolution of my marriage when my uncertainty as to its cause was the very rock upon which it had foundered? Was her affair with Hallie some kind of twisted fantasy I'd concocted to escape Bethany's unbearable ocean of tears? How could I get hung up on that part of the story without losing momentum as I sped toward reconciliation and redemption? What was forgiveness, anyway, and who did I need to forgive, and for what, before I could even get to the part about Ryan's killer? I didn't have time to figure it out. There was too much to do.

Some guy just commandeered a school bus. Twenty-eight third graders turned into hamburger by the extraordinary lethality of the killer's assault rifle. The .223 slug has three times the muzzle velocity of a bullet from my pistol. It hits with twice the impact and the shock wave it generates is like an explosion inside the body. Inside those 28 little bodies. My crimes have been erased by worse crimes, at least as far as the newspapers are concerned.

What if they *don't* catch me? What if I send this manifesto to the newspapers and they reject it as the work of a crank, an impostor?

As it turned out, I didn't have to spend Labor Day in one of Walter's straitjackets because I'd gotten quite busy with a very special gun-related research project. Just for kicks (I told myself at first, easing into it) I took a road trip down to Louisiana, as if it were a book-buying adventure, to check out Senator Morton Sawtelle's digs. Two twelve-hour days behind the wheel. Effortless for a driver of my experience. And I was highly motivated.

Nice white house on a couple of acres southwest of Baton Rouge, just a stone's throw from his state office. The summer recess on Capitol Hill was underway, so I got to see quite a bit of the ole' Morton at ribbon-cutting ceremonies, town hall meetings, and personal appearances at Rotary Clubs and Chamber of Commerce gatherings across the state. Chubby, perpetually smiling, with a boyish flop of hair over his forehead. A back-slapper of the old school, and tremendously energetic. They're not like us.

Touchingly, though he hopped around Louisiana with something approaching avidity, he was a homebody at heart. Back to Highland Road nearly every night. Pat the dog, tuck the kids in, hug the wife (as bosomy a belle as you could imagine). Oh, how they'd miss him!

Took the long way home, up Route 65, around Nashville, then north on Route 71 on the other side of Louisville, through Kentucky, and across the Ohio River into Indiana, to the town of Vevay (locals call it "Veevee") where, according to Truthfinder, dwelt Henry Becker, chief-in-charge of the NRA noise machine. Interesting country. Wine country, so they said. They said "quaint" and "historic," too, though I thought "hardscrabble" and "passed-over" would do just as well.

Becker's NRA office in Indianapolis was a two-hour schlep by limo, so during the week he stayed in a condo up there. But he was home most every weekend according to Benny, his yard man who, on a hunch, I followed late one afternoon, from Becker's place off in the woods on Cogley Cole Road, to a bar in downtown Vevay where, without appearing to be anything more than a slightly wet-brained wine tourist, I was able to buy him a beer and engage him in the usual bar room bullshit, culminating with me opining that Mr. Becker must be into huntn' n' fishin', given that his house was more or less in the middle of the woods, and that there didn't seem to be much else to do in Vevay anyway. Benny reckoned as, given Mr. Becker's day job, he probbly was, and that was that.

I spent Labor Day weekend in the woods overlooking the Becker estate, where the extended family had gathered. Younger adults, probably children. No wife that I could see. Four little Beckers, or whomevers, certainly grandchildren, cavorting around the pool out back. It was a lovely weekend, except for the bugs.

Then home, exhausted. Had I slept at all? A blurry week of zolpidem hallucinations. When the air cleared, I realized this was just like writing *Goodbye, My Son*. Go out on the road, gather my information. Come home, crash, rejuvenate, repeat.

Arthur Freedman was pathologically secretive and had concealed his whereabouts from Truthfinder, Intelius, and all the other online people-hunters. Undaunted, determined, and missile-like, I'd spent a good part of the summer failing to find him. Then, as I was recovering from my road trip, the answer came to me unbidden, as it had so many times before. I picked up the phone and called Cliff at Americans Together— why hadn't I thought of it sooner? (Why had I thought of it at all?) I told him I was writing an article on the gun industry and needed some personal information about Arthur Freedman, daddy of the infamous Gaboon Viper assault rifle.

Long pause. "We're, uh, not actually set up to find that kind of information, Joe."

"Your people did a pretty thorough job with Vicky Gimble."

"Hmm... We send those jobs out, if you know what I mean."

"I know exactly what you mean. And that's all I want, Cliff. Just somebody who can help me the way he helps you. By the way, have you read my book yet?"

That was the master stroke. The ease with which things were falling into place convinced me—not that I had any doubts before—of the rightness of my cause. Cliff put me in touch with a guy named Sanders who, like my old publicist, existed only as a telephone voice. Unlike the publicist, however, he had no sense of humor and no interest whatsoever in my made-up story about doing research for an article on... In fact, that was the very point at which he shut me up.

"I don't discuss these matters over the phone," he told me. "Cliff's recommendation is good enough for me. What I want you to do is mail a $1500 non-refundable retainer and very specific instructions to— have you got a pencil and paper?"

A week later I received, by registered mail, all I needed to know about Arthur Freedman. He had residences on Manhattan's upper east side (an entire building), a villa in Spoleto, Italy, and an estate in Kent, Connecticut. The first two might as well have been on Mars as far as my purposes were concerned. And Kent was something of a puzzler.

Freedman's place—palace—was off Route 7, right on the edge of a forest preserve, overlooking a lake. It seemed occupied; people came and went. But there was never a sign of Ratface, unless, ratlike, he came and went by night. Did he even live there? Three weekends in September without a trace of him. Gorgeous days, except for the last two, when the leftovers of Hurricane Izzy (Really?) made life miserable for everyone. Then the light bulb lit.

According to Sanders's report, Freedman had two sons, aged 14 and 16, enrolled in Hotchkiss School, about ten miles north of Kent. This 8,000 square-foot mansion was just a place to drop their suitcases. Would I have to wait until graduation to catch sight of him? Did the Ratfamily gather here for holidays? I was certain that a way would present itself. I would have my moment with Arthur Freedman.

Whatever it takes, as we used to say in Americans Together.

On good days when I wasn't absorbed in my very special gun-related research project, I'd haul my load of ecstasy down to the range at the Sportsman's Club and transfer it, via pistol (I'd recently upsized to a vintage all-steel Sig Sauer P229 chambered in .40 caliber), to rectangles of paper with a familiar image printed upon them. I was happy to group eight of ten shots in the center of Freedman's forehead from 35 or 40 feet. Think that's easy? Try it.

The shooting soothed me, which was good, because there were important tactical issues to be considered. I wear ear muffs over ear plugs on the range, so I mostly feel, rather than hear, the gunshots around me. This puts me in a removed, meditative, frame of mind, conducive to deep thinking. Thus it was that, one day shortly before my road trip to Louisiana, I had my final epiphany.

Unless I were a suicidal killer, which I most certainly was not, my pistol, no matter how expertly I wielded it, was not the tool for the job. However, as I looked around the range at the guys playing with their Colts, Armalites, .223 Remingtons, and similar assault rifles I felt, surprisingly, the disdain I used to feel in my days as an uneducated gun-grabbing bigot. These infantile jerks were getting their rocks off waving scary-looking death machines around. That revolted me. Then I thought of Andy Willets and forced myself to look again.

Actually, they weren't waving the things around; that kind of behavior would get them thrown off the range. They were carefully, ceremoniously almost, showing their toys to one another, marveling over the seemingly infinite variety the AR's modular design afforded. The shooting was calm, considered—at least until the finger-squeezing orgy began which, let's face it, is fun!

These guys, I had to admit, were more like me than not. They were getting off on the very thing that got me off that first time, on this very range, when that .22 casing found its way into the pocket of my vest. Assault rifles are terrifying things, designed solely and specifically to kill and wound as many people as possible, as efficiently as possible. And here were these working stiffs, family men most of them, perpetually aggrieved at being trapped witless in the mighty system, handling the instruments of death, mastering them, in a manner that could only be understood as *transgressive*.

Fathers of school-murdered sons were not supposed to be knowledgeable gun owners. Regular fellows were not supposed to be playing with, and customizing, the tools of mass slaughter. But I was, and they were. The effect in both cases was steroidal.

But if these guys were more or less like me, what was the cause of the contempt I was experiencing? Because the feeling sure wasn't going away (frightening image of my pistol hand, like Peter Sellers's hand in *Dr. Strangelove*, moving of its own accord).

I looked to my right, where a red-bearded young fellow was raising one of those death machines to his shoulder. It was a Smith and Wesson M&P Sport—one of the cheaper models. No more than a toy, really, and yet it looked as deadly, and in fact was as deadly, as any of the other ARs on the range. These things were meant for SEALS and SWAT teams. They had no place in civilian life, no utility—unless you used them to commit mass murder. And yet Freedman and his boys pumped them out by the tens of millions merely to satisfy the transgressive urges of a cohort of pathologically frustrated white males.

Assault rifles in civilian hands had no integrity. They were props in a fantasy, pieces of a video game delusion. I regarded my pistol which, after my Peter

Sellers moment, I had set on the counter in front of me, barrel downrange. It seemed succinct, functional, almost dignified in contrast to the silly Star Wars toys arrayed around it. If you had to protect yourself in the (exceedingly unlikely, statistically minuscule) event of an assault or a home invasion, a couple of .40 caliber hollow points delivered at close range by a semi-automatic pistol would do the job just fine. By contrast, can you imagine walking down the street with a Heckler Koch 417 under your coat? An AK-47 on top of the night stand beside your bed? Thirty rounds to kill a deer? Flagrant and ridiculous in their menace, these guns were no more than props for Second Amendment drama queens.

Which left me in a bit of a bind, armament wise.

Then Roger came into my life. He was an elk hunter, a retired veterinarian. We met at a Sportman's Club Sunday breakfast, and I courted him with more ardor than I'd courted Vicky. We were going elk hunting in Idaho!

It turned out I had a knack for the sport—a steady hand and a keen eye, the residue, no doubt, of my brutish and short days as a Marine. Roger de-flinched me on the range with a .22 and loaned me one of his competition rifles to improve my skills. With his customized Weatherby Mark V he could drop a dozen rounds onto a target the size of a pie plate 1000 yards out. I was never more than a talented amateur, but that was all I needed to be. In short order I was proud owner of a Gunwerks LR1000, a sort of Cadillac of long-distance rifles, equipped with a 5.5-22x50mm G7 Nightforce scope, rock solid at anything inside half a mile. Blam! No more black.

Then it was Halloween. (Our town, I'm proud to say, ignored the new-age Saturday observance and stuck with the real day.) I left the front light on and sat at Hank's desk, and I could hear the little spooks and goblins laughing and screaming up and down the street. But not a one of them came to the door of the Book Palace. Too genuinely scary, I guess. I noticed that the guy across the street packed his two boys—Batman and a Storm Trooper (Star Wars, not Hitler)—into his SUV and drove off with them, presumably to a friendlier neighborhood. I ate about six of those miniature Milky Way bars myself. The first one was delicious, far better than I remembered Milky Way bars tasting. Then I couldn't stop.

After nobody had finished coming to my door, I turned on the Thursday night football game and was surprised to see Wendel Atkins in a special halftime feature, sitting on a couch across from some sports announcer and a vaguely familiar football player. They were talking about the plague of gun violence! I remembered Wendel from Americans Together events. His daughter Bernadette was the one who'd been assassinated on the set of Celebrity Bingo. Tens of millions watched the crazed cameraman approach her, standing beside the giant numbers pot as was her wont. (She was one of the three gorgeous numbers callers.) She knew him, obviously. She extended her hand to him. "Bill! This is a surprise." (Her last words!) Was he going to propose? Wacky things were always happening on Celebrity Bingo so neither she nor the audience was particularly surprised by this sudden improvisation. Until he took the revolver out, it was a snub-nosed .38, and shot her twice in the chest at point-blank range. The camera followed her to the floor; we were still thinking it was some kind of prank. Then we heard another shot off camera—him blowing his brains out—and everything went black.

Which was how Wendel became a poster parent for Americans Together, replacing the poor mother whose son had been shot *by his own eighth grade teacher*, and who, in turn, replaced the daughter of that heroic mall cop who lost his life taking down the mall shooter in Santa Fe. Americans Together worked them hard, but it wasn't exploitation. Some people need so desperately for the murder of their loved ones to have meaning that they are willing to subject themselves to media jackals in the hope that a public display of their agony will inspire the nation to do something about its causes.

Interestingly, these people hardly ever burn out. It's more the case that the American public burns out on them. Which is why Americans Together keeps putting new people up there.

The televised Celebrity Bingo shooting got the most hits ever on YouTube (which inspired my combustible hopes, initially, for a gun commercial starring Richard Winters), even though it was only up there for a short while before the YouTube people took it down. Pirated clips kept appearing and they'd be taken down, soon to be replaced by more of the same. Talk about viral! This was definitely a case of YouTube subscribers telling the censors where to get off. But wasn't it odd that a televised murder should be the occasion for such a protest?

Not necessarily. Not if you held to Vicky's theory of the commodification of gun violence news, or Andy's cynical advance of her theory (as proved by that awful Facebook suicide epidemic)—that shootings were the ultimate in reality TV. As I sat, bathed in the blue glow of the tube, listening to Wendel and his interlocutors talking softly about hideous things, surrounded by my Milky Way wrappers, swirling my melted ice dregs of a highball, waiting for the third quarter to begin, I could hear America whisper, in a whisper she could barely stand to hear, *at least it wasn't my kid*—revolting thought that it is, that even *having* it is. Impatient for the game, needing the spectacle of drugged gladiators concussing themselves to efface those suffering parents, and the hideous cause of their suffering, and the even more hideous fact that we're not going to do a damned thing about it except shamefacedly thank our lucky stars we aren't them.

All those dead third graders, and young men and women, and good boys who loved their mamas, buried way down deep inside us, and there go Wendel and the announcer and that linebacker for the Bears, whatever his name is, pitching their hopeless pitch, and Bernadette, too. Adios, Bernadette! Replaced by a Ford truck commercial.

It came to me that night that what we need to do, if we really want to bring about change in the gun violence situation, is to seize on the cognitive dissonance evoked by the gruesome murder of Bernadette Atkins, and recognize it rather than deny it. Recognize it and enhance it in order to become energized by it. I thought of all the raggedy skeletons and zombies and gorillas and super heroes running through the dusk in the street outside the Book Palace. Ghosts of Halloween ghosts from Ryan's day, mimicking, in their innocent way, the original Halloween rising of the real ghosts of Ryan, and the kiddies killed in the Bouncy Castle and at those schools and theaters and malls, and on ghetto streets.

What we need to do is call those dead kids up from their graves, by the hundreds of thousands, gory and stinking and rotten, and snap them like a pistol in America's face. Like the crime scene photo of Shannon's bullet-riddled corpse. *This is what you're paying for your Second Amendment rights.*

April 20, I Think

I began this account with the intention of demonstrating the forces that impinged upon me, transforming me from an average Joe to the very embodiment of the problem of gun violence in America (And its solution!), repaying monstrosities with monstrosities. When people understand why what happened happened, it will happen again. It will. And again. Until America rises in agony and cries *Enough!*

The fact that I have told my story incrementally, episode by scattered episode, implies a progression or, to use the phrase favored by gun nuts everywhere, a "slippery slope." Well, time might move forward by ticks, but by that Halloween night I wasn't progressing anywhere; I'd long since gotten there.

The symptoms of my affliction subsided once again. The headaches and depression disappeared; the terrible roaring quieted, and the intensity of the ecstatic interludes diminished to mere exuberance. There was only a residual trace of inflammation, which exhibited itself in unsurprising ways—my ongoing inability, for example, to stop wondering how come crazed gunmen never went after rats like Arthur Freedman or Henry Becker. It was complicated. Or, I should say, complex. A progression is complicated; a system is complex. And, as I've been at pains to explain to you, this was more in the nature of an epiphany than a progression. An instantaneous and complete vision of the monstrosity of the mighty system.

In the weeks between Halloween and Thanksgiving I managed, with a little effort, to reduce my whiskey/zolpidem/oxycodone intake but was forced, as a result, to endure an interlude of muddleheadedness, during which time, instead of asking the library about the $4500 they still owed me for the crazy whaling captain's journal, as I resolved to do each morning, or working on my redemption memoir for Daniel as I resolved to do each afternoon, I wound up sitting at Hank's desk, looking out the window at leaf tornadoes and left-over ghosts of Halloween ghosts, trapped in tightly-wound thought loops, as above, regarding the lack of psycho gun-industry killers—though, as I'm sure you understand by now, there was a core of reason to it— and, finally, as the fog lifted each evening at cocktail hour, gathering the thoughts that eventually resulted in my setting these words down, or herding the electrons that make the pixels that form the words, since I was using Hank's computer and then my new one, rather than Senator Perkins's yellow legal pad to do the job.

The vortex passed on. I don't need to talk about it any longer. I need more ice.

Nor is there any use in boring you, more than I already have, with the obsessive details of my preparations as the dark days approached, picking the scab I'd become, unable to stop. The elk hunter and I parted ways. A silly argument over nothing. You know how those things are.

Then I did stop. I drew a breath, breathing good air in, just the way you would before the trigger squeezed itself, and I understood that my murderous fantasies about Freedman, Sawtelle and Becker were no more than that. Mere fantasies. Simply part of the healing process or, to put it more ornately, an aspect of my journey through the vortex, the pilgrimage that would result in my being healed. Two weeks? Ten months? All I had to do was endure.

It had been crazy to want to kill the ones with their hands on the levers, and their stooges, and the political vermin who did the bidding of the stooges.

Literally crazy. And pointless and stupid. If I assassinated them, as I'd so carefully planned, one by one, Freedman touring his estate (he was, in fact, "home for Christmas"), Sawtelle scratching his ass and picking the morning paper off the sidewalk in front of his house, Becker with his donkey-smile, pausing to greet the limo driver... All the research I'd done, the contingencies I'd accommodated, the locations I'd scouted, the cunning angles, the patient concealment. Blam!

If, as I was saying, I assassinated these despicable individuals—even in the name of every victim of gun violence—they'd only become martyrs. The dead would not come back to life. We survivors would not be avenged. The situation would become even more polarized, and nobody would have learned a thing. It had been a foolish notion. I felt great shame. I felt a madman's shame.

As the day of Ryan's murder drew near, I dreaded calling Bethany. Surely she wouldn't bring Rex to the graveyard. But what if she did? Then it was December 15th, the can't-there-be-a-better-word-than-anniversary day, and she had not called, and I had not called her. My way was clear. At dawn I spread some boughs of balsam fir over Ryan's grave and headed south. Six days, 3400 miles. Sawtelle, Becker, Freedman, in that order. Flawless. Despite that long wait in the snow at Freedman's. Everything happening for a reason.

Once I had him in my sights it took all the resolve I could muster to resist blowing Sawtelle to bits. But

I held true to my higher purpose and slid the scope a few feet to his right, to the forehead of his son. Obviously, the thing to do was to go for their children. Well, Freedman's and Sawtelle's children. Becker had grandchildren. One of them had to die, as well. The youngest, most innocent. It was a terrible shame. That first shot made me vomit.

But the only way to reach them was through their kids. How else were they going to understand where we were coming from?

If I hadn't done it, one of the others would have.

"After college I spent four years in the Navy, reading Pound and then Olson and, of course, the dozens of writers those giants insisted one must have familiarity with—before even thinking of adding a word to the conversation. Oh, I aspired to those heights! But time carried me to a different place. I'm an antiquarian book dealer *and* a writer, so I've got the best of both worlds.

I began in the bookselling trade in 1976 and had been an inveterate scribbler since the 1960s, but I didn't become a writer until 1999. Sadly ("ironically" doesn't seem apt here), I'm a writer because my son Galen was killed in a school shooting in 1992. In the wake of this event, to keep from harming or killing myself or anyone else, I determined to pour my energies into answering the question foremost on everyone's mind— mine foremost—"How could this have happened?"

A lengthy and therapeutic investigation led to my first book, *Gone Boy*, followed by four more books. And now this calm, demented one."

* 9 781956 005905 *